Fish Angel
and
Other Stories

Fish Angel
and
Other Stories

Cathy Worthington

Printed in the United States of America
First Printing, 2020

ISBN: 978-1-7363075-0-2 (paperback)
ISBN: 978-1-7363075-1-9 (ebook)

Cover and Interior Design: Creative Publishing Book Design

With thanks to Carolyn Wheat
for years of writing help

Contents

Jackson's Eagle

The sound of my deck chair scraping the weathered planks jars the fragile silence. I drag it over to my favorite spot in front of the railing. Grasping the splintery arm with one hand and a can of Bud with the other, slowly I let myself down. Halfway, my knees give out and I drop with a plop. Beer sloshes all over the place. I brush a few drops off my pant leg and settle back. The Bud's nice and ice cold and makes my teeth ache. The air's hot and smells of sagebrush and wild mountain thyme. I stroke the stubble on my chin and gaze up at the sky, letting the stillness enfold me. For just a brief moment I stop feeling the pain.

A hundred or so feet below me the Madison River winds its way through the shallow valley, the ripples of its dark waters shooting off silvery sparks of light. From here you can follow its path east through the yellow-green meadows and into the

1

distance where the snowy peaks of the Yellowstone mountains rise up. In the early evening sunshine they've turned that pastel color that all the western landscape painters try to capture but never really can. Automatically my focus shifts to the right, up-river about a hundred yards to where a dead elm stands by itself just down the embankment from a clump of pines. Sure enough. There on its highest branch perches my buddy, an American bald eagle. They used to be endangered, but in Montana they're coming back. He'll stay that way for hours, a white-hooded sentry, only his head moving. In profile, you can see the outline of his beak. Louise said he guards the river. I never argued the point. I raise my beer can to salute him. This is his river. This is his realm.

His wings unfold and rise. He leans forward and shoves off. Going fishing. I've watched him do it a million times before. He swoops down toward the river and glides just a few feet above. He'll snag himself a trout double the size any of the fly fishermen can catch. He puts those assholes to shame.

His wings flap hard. He rises in a steep arc and banks my way. Here he comes. My God, he's never come this close. He's almost overhead. Wingspan's gotta be at least eight feet. I can feel the beat of his wings. Rising halfway out of my chair, I shout, "Louise, you gotta come out and see this." I sink back down as I realize. She can't come out. She can't come see this. She can't because she is no more.

I grit my teeth as the familiar ache settles over me. God, for a second there it was as if she *was* still alive, as if I could call to her and she *would* come out. How long before my mind will stop playing these tricks on me?

I shake my head as I watch the eagle flap off. Wish I could soar off into the sunshine. I'd take off and never come back. About a month ago I thought of doing just that. Climbed to a place high above the river. Big ol' butte that jutted out over the water. It was a weekday. No tourists. No fly fishermen. Not a soul around. I must have been about a hundred yards above the water. Thought I'd cast myself off. Soar out over the silvery ripples, catch an updraft into that big blue Montana sky. Lost my nerve, though. Couldn't do it. Stumbled backwards and landed on my ass. That night I stood in front of the bathroom mirror staring at my sagging chest with its measly sprinkle of white hairs. "You poor slob, you haven't got the guts."

I sink further into my chair and try thinking about not thinking. Try to let myself drift off into the silence that surrounds me. When I open my eyes, the eagle's casing the river again. He swoops down, and just as his talons are skimming the water a dory full of fly fishermen appears around the bend. God damn it, they're going to ruin his kill. They ought to ban humans on this river. Sure enough, the eagle sweeps back into the sky without his fish. I reach for the railing and yank myself to my feet. Waving my fist like some lunatic I holler,

"Hey, you guys down there. You just scared the eagle." Three blank faces look up. From a hundred feet away I can't read their expressions. I don't need to. The middle fingers tell it all.

Used to be fly fishermen in Montana were a high class group. Lots of camaraderie. Not any more. Louise loved the sport. I taught her to tie her own flies. I can just see her now, sitting at the kitchen table, arthritic fingers working those tiny, intricate knots—brow creased, lips tight, breath held. Another image of her flashes before me as the dory slips out of sight. I see her standing on that grassy green sand bar down below, a cutthroat dangling from her line. There's a big grin on her face and sunshine in her eyes.

The sound of someone knocking barely reaches my ears. Slowly I rise and shuffle into the house. Now, who'n hell could be coming over at five p.m. on a Sunday night? Who'n hell could be coming over period? I don't have any friends in Montana—at least not anymore. Then I remember. The pastor from the little church in Ennis, Louise's pastor. He phoned the other day and asked if I'd like to go fishing. I told him I don't fish anymore. Fishing, my ass. He just wants to get me in a boat and start talking religion to me. Probably wants my money. They're all alike.

I sneak into the guest bedroom and peek through a crack in the curtain. A male voice hollers out my name. Then silence. I hold my breath and tiptoe back into the family room.

"Jackson?" It's my name again only this time it's coming from the deck. I catch a quick glimpse of Louise's preacher through the window before I duck behind the couch. Feel kind of foolish hiding like this, a little juvenile you might say, but, hell, I'm in no mood to face that preacher. Had enough of his type when Louise was dying—those young bright-faced hospice pastors who always sound cheery and upbeat. What'n hell do they know about dying? My legs are going to sleep. I bring my right index finger to my mouth and attempt to extract a splinter with my teeth. A trio of dust bunnies peek out at me from under the end table. There's something gritty on the floor beneath my left hand—probably rat scat.

Footsteps enter the room. "Jackson?" I don't move an inch. Jesus, it sure would be embarrassing if this guy caught me like this. I can just hear Louise now: "You ought to be ashamed of yourself, Jackson." Well, I am. A little. But not enough to socialize with this preacher. After what seems like forever I hear him clomp back out to the deck and go around the side of the house. I crawl to a new position so he won't see me through the window as he goes by. I hear his pickup's engine start up. Feeling stiff and more than a little guilty, I struggle to my feet, go into the kitchen, and fix myself a good, strong scotch. I even pour a little on the hole in my finger where the splinter was.

I'm just getting ready to take my drink and go back out to the deck when the cell phone tinkles its stupid little tune. I check the name. Sure enough, it's Pastor Elliot. Bet my daughter's the one who's been putting him up to bugging me. She's been driving me crazy all summer long. "You shouldn't be up at the cabin by yourself, Dad. I worry. Why don't you come on home?" No way. I'm not leaving until the snow's waist high. I glance at the photo on the kitchen counter—my daughter with the four grandboys. Last time she called she threatened to bring the whole unruly bunch up here.

I sit back down and gaze out at the river. My wife's voice haunts me. "Jackson, you need to stop this silliness. You can't just shut yourself off from humanity." She used to try to get me to accompany her to church. I'd do just about anything for her, but that. She believed in such crazy stuff, like the spirits of the dead invading birds and animals—used to think the scrub jay that begged for peanuts at our window sill was her dead aunt.

Movement on my side of the river catches my eye. I rise to my feet so I can get a better look. It's the eagle. He couldn't be more than fifty feet below me. Clutched in his talons, still flopping away, is the biggest silveriest, slipperiest ol' cutthroat you ever did see. The eagle begins tearing at the fish's flesh with his beak. Suddenly he stops and raises his head, full alert, his eyes darting everywhere. Man, he's got a scary look about him. You wouldn't want to mess with him, that's for sure. His wings spread and he starts beating the air. Oh, shit, now I see why. Down the river, about a quarter of a mile away, here comes a grizzly bear, barreling full speed ahead. The eagle's gonna try and take off, but I don't know how in hell he'll be able to with that big ol' trout in his talons. The grizzly's just a few hundred yards away when the eagle manages to get airborne, the fish dangling from just one claw. God almighty, no one's ever going to believe this. Hell, *I* wouldn't believe it.

The eagle heads up my way. If only I had a video camera. He's just a couple of feet above me, so close I could almost reach up and touch his wing when all of a sudden that damn fish comes loose from his claw. Splat. It lands right in the middle of my deck. Spikes of adrenalin sting the hairs on my arms. A bird of prey about to land on my deck, the most dangerous bear in Montana just down the hill—everything is happening too fast. The eagle swoops high into an arc, circles around, and heads back my way. I glance toward the house trying to estimate how quickly I can make it across the deck to the sliding glass door. Wouldn't you know, it's closed. Force of habit. Louise always insisted on it. You don't want to let a mosquito in. Otherwise it'll buzz you all night long.

I've barely taken a step when I see the bear trampling through the fire weed and columbine, just a few yards from my deck. There's no time. Oh, God, should I run? Should I stay where I am? I move behind a chaise and in my panic manage to pin myself between it and the window. The bear practically rips my railing off, climbing over—big ol' sonofabitch, must be over a thousand pounds. His flesh jiggles like lard, but don't let that fool you, he's all muscle. He goes for the fish first, gets it in his mouth and lifts his head. That's when he senses my presence. With a roar, he drops the fish and rises on his hind legs. He's at least seven feet tall and so close I can actually smell his scent, a wild, rank odor of river bottom and rotting fish and pine.

Holy, Jesus, my knees are shaking. The sliding door is only a few feet away, but the bear is closer to it than I am. What do they say? Never run from a bear? Stand tall and wave your arms? Make yourself look big? No, that's for black bears. What was the advice about grizzlies? Oh, now I remember: *Forget it, man, you're dead meat.*

As I stand there looking into this bear's coal black eyes, every prayer I've never prayed comes to mind. My insides turn to liquid. Weird thoughts circulate through my head, my mother kissing me good-bye on the first day of school, the glow in my Dad's eyes when I was awarded my eagle scout, sitting back with the coffins of dead comrades on my way back from Vietnam, the sight of Louise's tousled blonde hair after the first time we made love, Janine, our beautiful, dimple-faced baby girl, Louise's last words, her dying breath. With my crazed sight I almost imagine that the bear cocks his head slightly, that his eyes soften. Then I remember—you're never ever supposed to look a bear in the eye. It challenges them. You do it, and they'll attack for sure.

What the hell, isn't this what I've been wishing for? Isn't this the easy way out?

Again the bear roars. Just as it does, the eagle swoops down and snatches at the top of the bear's head with its talons. The bear stumbles backwards and sits down with a thump that makes the deck shake. The eagle banks to the left and circles around for a second pass. Metal screeches against wood as I shove the chaise out of my way. Moving in what seems like slow motion, I make it to the sliding glass door, slip inside, and slide it closed. My legs give out. With a motion like limp spaghetti, I drop to the floor. Heart's fibrillating to beat the band. Know I ought to go get my shotgun, but I'm too weak. I lean against the side of the couch and close my eyes. The world goes blank.

When I open my eyes, there's no sign of either the bear or the eagle. First I go get my Remington, then quietly and slowly I open the sliding glass door. No sign of the fish either. Glancing from side to side I step out onto the deck. Way up off to the right my white-hooded sentry sits perched on his branch. He was guarding more than the river tonight.

In the distance an eighteen wheeler groans as it shifts gears going up hill. I pull out my cell phone and study it for a minute. Maybe I'll give my daughter a call after all. Time those grandboys learned how to fish.

Back To Sea

Paddleboard under one arm, I start down the sidewalk toward the bay. At the top of broken cement steps that lead down to the sand, I pause. A weekday, and the beach is empty. Everyone's at work. Everyone but me.

The bay stretches out before me, calm and flat as the surface of a mirror. It's the only place I could think of to come today that wouldn't bring pain. Staying at home sure wasn't an option. My wife, Jackie, her eyes bleeding sympathy, couldn't stop with the comments. They were supposed to make me feel better. They didn't.

Laid off.

It felt like the world was coming to an end.

At the bottom of the stairs my golden retriever Hal takes a leak on his favorite clump of daisies. I descend a few steps

11

until my feet touch sand just beginning to warm from the morning sun. A dark line delineates the previous night's high tide mark. Beside a collapsing sandcastle lies a blue plastic shovel and a pink flowered pail. We used to bring our kids to this beach all the time, but now that they're teenagers, they're into surfing. "Kellogg's Beach is for babies," my son complains. For me, Kellogg's Beach is the most peaceful place on earth.

My paddleboard makes a hollow sound as I drop it onto the water. Slowly, Hal limps over. Standing knee-deep, I push the board so that one end touches the sand. "Here, boy." I pat the rough spot where he always sits. He touches the board with his paw then draws it back.

"C'mon, boy." I pat the board again. Getting on is always a balancing act, and he's balked before, but not like this.

I shake my head. "Aw, c'mon, pal. Don't be getting old on me. Not today. I can't take it." A few more tentative tries with the paw, then Hal gives a little leap and lands splay-legged on the board. He barely whimpers, but I know it must have hurt. The vet said his arthritis is getting pretty bad. I pat his head. "It's okay, boy. We're all getting up there." Would anyone want to hire a guy of fifty-two?

Carefully I step onto the board and juggle my weight to get my balance. I dip the paddle into the water, first on the left, then on the right, gliding us gently out of the yacht basin toward the tip of Shelter Island. A hint of jet fuel from

Lindbergh Field drifts my way. Warm airflow from the east—we're having a Santa Ana. Above me the sky is cloudless and brilliant blue, another sign of a high-pressure system. They'd said on the news it might reach ninety by noon.

"What say we go scare some seals off the bait barges, Hal?"

His tail flops his approval.

Just off to our left a v-formation of pelicans skims the water barely inches above the surface.

As we near the bait docks, the water becomes a churning cauldron of dark, glistening bodies. The barking is deafening. Hal lets out a few woofs, but mostly he just watches, his tail twitching, his paws shuffling to keep balance on the tippy board. Seals scramble on and off the bait barges, their slippery bodies gleaming in the sunlight. Pelicans the size of Hal pace the wooden planks, challenging the seals and us with their red-eyed glares.

A fishing boat stops by to pick up bait. One of them gestures at the board and me. "It's a tough life," he shouts.

Normally my response would be, "Yeah, but someone's gotta do it." Not today.

I watch the crew load squid into the bait tank at the back of their boat. The smell in the air is the one I love, of fish and dried seaweed and hot tar. The water sparkles in the sunlight.

What a day to be heading out to sea. I watch with envy as the fishing boat chugs off. I'd give anything to be living that kind of life. I wonder what it pays—not enough to support a wife and a mortgage and two college-bound teenagers, that's for sure.

A gust of wind sends ripples across the water, a harbinger of Santa Ana winds about to pick up. They'll be right in our face as we head homeward. It took about 20 minutes to get out here, but it'll take double that to get back.

I try to concentrate on the stroke-stroke of the paddle, try not to think of anything else. God, it feels good to be using my muscles instead of my mind. It makes me want to do a 180 and head straight out to sea. Stroke, stroke. All the way to Hawaii.

Before I hear the sound, I sense the presence. It's like when you're in a dark room and you get the feeling that someone else is in there with you. A great whoosh, and not more than ten yards off my bow, is the crusty topside of a giant gray whale. Gently the curve of its spine slides back under the water. A few seconds later it surfaces again and blows. The mist from its spray hangs in the air, fishy and rank like the smell of the bait barges.

"Jesus, Hal." My voice rises to a squeak. "Did you see that?"

Hal paws the board and barks frantically. Suddenly he's that young dog again.

This time the whale's fluke comes all the way out of the water. It's diving for the bottom. Behind on the surface it leaves a circle of flat water, the unmistakable footprint of a whale. Amazing. When it went under, it didn't even set up a ripple to rock our board.

I begin paddling using long, strong strokes, pushing us ahead at maximum speed. A few seconds pass and the whale surfaces again, just off to our right at about two o'clock. "Oh, man," I whisper. "No one's gonna believe this."

I pant and stroke, and there's the whale again. A few minutes more, and its entire head comes out of the water. Spy hopping. I've observed it before in nature videos, but never in real life. I see its eye and what looks like a smile on its great, wide mouth. I can just hear my buddies when I tell them. *Whales can't smile.* Bullshit. This one can.

*   *   *

"It was unbelievable, Jackie." I take a big swig of my Bud, then set it down. "It stayed with us all the way in as far as Shelter Island. I mean, all the way. Can you believe it? Then some fuckin' cigar boat came along, and it dove. Geez, a whale in the bay."

My wife turns from the counter where she's been slicing tomatoes. "Did you get a chance to update your resume?" The years have added specks of gray to her brunette hair, but the vertical lines between her eyebrows are brand new.

15

With a sigh I slide off the stool, turn, and head for our office.

"Aw, honey," she yells after me. "I'm sorry. I didn't mean to make you feel bad."

Everything makes me feel bad.

*   *   *

Morning comes, accompanied by blue skies and sunshine. With an imaginary shotgun pointed at the back of my head, I sit down at the computer and tackle the chore of updating my resume. I've sent it out to six places, including a company in Tulsa. Tulsa. Oh, God. There's no way I'd be able to stand living that far from the ocean. What if that turns out to be the only company that says *yes*? Can I do it? For my family I'll have to.

Two weeks pass, and not a word in response to my job hunt, but practically every day there's something in the newspaper or on TV about the whale. They've even given it a name, "Diego," named after San Diego Bay. It's been spotted daily over by the Embarcadero and someone even reported seeing it as far in as the Coronado Bay Bridge.

*   *   *

"Anything?"

I jerk around to see Jackie standing in the door to our office. Quickly I minimize the game of Spider Solitaire I've been playing. I level her with what I hope is an innocent gaze. "Nothing." Our savings is down around twenty thousand. At the rate we're used to spending, that won't last more than a couple of months. I haven't told her, but I've been thinking about putting the house on the market. I stand and squeeze past her and head down the hall. "Where're you going?" she calls after me.

"Down to the bay." I step into the garage and close the back door before I can hear her response. *Be a jerk,* I tell myself. *Just be a goddamned jerk.*

When I get down to Kellogg's, I notice two whale watching boats in the channel just off Shelter Island. They aren't moving which means the whale must be somewhere close by. "Come on, Hal," I shout. "Let's get going."

Just as we're paddling past the coastguard station, I sense its presence. Then comes the familiar whoosh, and, sure enough, there's the whale, dead ahead. A power boat swerves our way, and all of a sudden I can see the whale's dark shape directly beneath us. If it surfaces now, it could come up under my board. I'd be killed and leave Jackie and the boys in a hell of a mess. I back-paddle fast.

As if this great creature can read my thoughts, it stays down. A few minutes later it surfaces a safe distance away. I start paddling, and it stays right with me. Intentional? It has to be.

*　　　*　　　*

A response from the last company on my job hunt straggles in. *No.*

I sit alone at the counter eating my dinner—leftover tuna casserole with a salad of iceberg lettuce and cheapo tomatoes—a far cry from the barbequed salmon with gourmet greens we're used to. Jackie's gone with the boys to watch our oldest play varsity basketball. I couldn't bear to go, couldn't deal with the other parents—all the empathetic smiles, the pats on the back, the *how's-it-going.* They think they understand, but they don't. Nobody does.

Across the room from me, Hal lies in his basket near the hearth. His arthritis has flared up recently, so much so that I've had to stop taking him out on the bay. It hurts me to look at him. My buddy. My best friend. His eyes lift and meet mine. *He* understands.

On TV the six o'clock news talks about the city's mayoral race, the Charger stadium controversy, a car accident on the 805. I sip my beer, half listening until— It's the word *whale* that catches my attention. It's come all the way into the yacht harbor this time and has just been spotted off Kellogg's Beach.

It's dark by the time I get down to the bay. People mill along the shoreline. Someone points to where the whale is swimming near Peckham's Pier. Why on earth is it coming into waters this shallow? Is it sick? Is it trying to beach itself? The lights from the boat docks on Shelter Island reflect off black ripples. A familiar soft whoosh, and I spot the whale's dark shape not more than fifteen yards from shore. It's so close. Too close. I'm as worried as I'd be if Hal were running into oncoming traffic. Everyone on the beach cheers. I pat the air, trying to shush them. The whale disappears, and the beach goes silent. Soft cries of disbelief rise as it re-appears just a few feet from shore. I could walk right into the water and touch it.

With a jerk I turn and race back up the sand to the stairs. My paddleboard is still on top of my SUV. I fiddle with the clamps on the rack. It's a crazy idea, but it just might work.

By the time I get back down to the water, the whale has disappeared. A sightseer stares at my board and me in my khakis and polo shirt. "You're not going out there, are you?" Before he can tell me what a fool I am, I kick off my shoes, slap my board onto the water, and am off. My heart pounds. I'm in such a small area, surrounded by docks and anchored boats, that there'd barely be room for a whale to move. If it comes up underneath me like it did the other day, things could get dicey. One slap from that mother of a tail and… *Don't think about it.*

I begin stroking, heading out of the yacht harbor toward the channel. "C'mon," I whisper. "Let's go for nice long swim." I glance around. The whale's nowhere in sight. I'm just getting ready to turn around when the familiar whoosh sounds.

Yes!

"C'mon," I whisper. At the tip of Shelter Island, I point my board toward the channel and open sea. The whale's followed me before. The big question is will it now? Spotlights blind me. Off to my left the sound of a powerboat's engine putters along. It has to be the news media.

I wave for them to back off. They move even closer. "You're breaking the Marine Mammal Protection Act," I shout. The law states that a vessel must not approach within a hundred yards of a whale. A fluke glistens in the spotlight. They've scared it. It's diving. I shake my fist. "I'm trying to get the whale out of the bay. Can't you assholes see that?"

"Are you nuts?" someone on the boat shouts.

"Fuck you," I yell back.

All of a sudden the boat's spotlight arcs skyward, then dives. "Was that the whale?" someone shouts. The disturbance sends waves in my direction. I bend my knees struggling to keep my balance. The news boat's had enough. It takes off leaving me bobbing up and down in its wake.

I wait for the water to calm before starting to paddle again, hoping, praying that the whale is still down there somewhere and that it will stay with me and let me show it the way. About five minutes passes. Nothing. Maybe those guys were right. Maybe I am nuts.

"C'mon," I pray. "I know you're down there."

Whoosh. A soft spray fills the air, and the mound of the whale's back appears glistening silver in the moonlight.

It's about three miles to the end of Point Loma and the open sea. I have no lights, which is against the law, not to mention dangerous as hell. I don't care. I just keep on paddling, shoulders aching, stroking against the tide. There's nothing left except me and the darkness and the whale. My paddle glides through the water. *Whoosh*. I can almost predict when the sound will come, as dependable as my own heartbeat.

A dark shape rises off the horizon. I ignore it and keep on paddling, the rhythm mesmerizing me. Stroke. Stroke. The shape is growing larger. Stroke. Stroke. The shape looms above me, at least two stories high.

Suddenly I realize where I am—right smack in the middle of the channel with an aircraft carrier bearing down on me. If it could see me it would be blasting its horn, but I have no lights. I turn right and paddle like hell. Seals on the channel marking buoys bark as I pass. "All hands prepare…" The hollow echo of an announcement being made on the carrier fills the air. Chest bursting, shoulders on fire, I keep on going. When I finally slow and look back, the carrier is just passing me with less than a hundred yards to spare. Any closer and I would have been sucked underneath it by the whirlpool from its engines.

Sweat pours off my forehead. My arms feel weak. My hands tremble. Jesus, I never should have tried this. There's no sign of the whale, and here I am almost out to sea without even a lifejacket. I don't know what else to do but keep on paddling.

I'm beyond Ballast Point now. A fresh breeze blows in my face causing me to shiver. I no longer have feeling in my feet. Closer and closer I come to the open sea, but still no sign of the whale. Did I lose it when the carrier came by?

I pick up the sound of waves breaking at the surfing beach near the end of the point. A light breeze ruffles the black water, turning its ripples silver. And that's when I see it. Way out there in front of me. The whale. It spouts, then dives, and disappears. It's headed for open seas. A few seconds later it re-appears. First its head, then its whole body, comes right out of the water. It lands with a great splash of froth that glows florescent in the moonlight. Again it jumps. Again and again. I whoop and holler, but there's no one around to hear me. Except the pelicans and a few seals.

Whether this is some kind of celebration on the whale's part I'll never know, but I like to think so. The last glimpse I get of my giant friend is its fluke glistening in the moonlight, a whale's good-bye.

*   *   *

I've just added a big slug of rum to my mug of tea when Jackie and the boys arrive home. The boys go on up to bed.

22

Jackie slips onto the stool beside me. She glances down at my damp khakis. "What happened to you?"

I take a sip of tea. "It's a long story."

She sighs. "Everyone missed you tonight."

"Uh hmm." I take another sip of my tea.

"Carl Owens said they might have an opening at Crown &—"

I open my arms and pull her in, stroking her hair, using my thumb to smooth the furrows between her eyebrows. "It's okay," I whisper. "We're going to be all right."

The moon angles down from the skylight over our heads, the same moon that gave me my last glimpse of my whale.

The House
at 5th and Salem

The house at 5th and Salem was built in 1883 by physician Oscar J. Stanley. He prided himself in many of its modern conveniences, such as the dumb waiter, and the laundry chutes from every bedroom, and the Otis elevator which ran from the basement all the way up to the third floor. In its glory days this Victorian mansion of Italianate design saw the weddings of four Stanley daughters and ten granddaughters. Babies were born in the canopied beds. There were ice-cream socials. Ladies arrived carrying parasols, dressed in gowns with high collars of fine lace.

A hundred years later and the surrounding elms have grown to towering heights, but, with the exception of the peeling paint, the weeds, and the bee bee holes in the leaded glass window on the third floor, very little about this Victorian mansion has really changed. Well, maybe one thing has. Oscar's pride and joy—the Otis—is now nothing more than a dark, empty chute. The elevator itself stopped working back in 1945. A bureau has been placed in front of the door on the third floor to prevent accidents.

In June of 1983, the mansion has one sole occupant, eighty-year-old Grace Stanley, a spinster and one of Oscar Stanley's last two surviving relatives. Grace suffers from severe osteoarthritis. Her knees have gotten so bad that these days she rarely ventures downstairs. She uses alcohol for the pain. Refuses to see a doctor. In fact, she refuses to leave the house at all. Occasionally she can be seen peering from a third story window. Neighbors who don't realize the mansion is occupied mistake her for a ghost.

* * *

When Phonecia Washington arrives at 5th and Salem each morning, she removes her slacks and shirt and puts on a white uniform, and everyday before she leaves, she changes back into her regular clothes. This particular morning is no different from any other. As always, she fixes Grace's breakfast tray then, huffing and puffing, she carries it up the three flights of stairs. Years ago the climb was nothing, but Phonecia's getting on sixty eight, has aches and pains of her own.

"Morning, Miss Stanley." She's careful to pronounce it *miss* and not *mz*. It's another case of Grace refusing to go along with the times just like her insistence on the white uniform.

Phonecia'd rather be hung from a tree than have anyone see her wearing it.

King George, Grace's cat, jumps from the bed and lands without a sound on the hooked rug. Grace slowly turns over and groans as she rises to a sitting position. Static has made a halo of her fine white hair. She scowls at Phonecia. "Where've you been? I've been waiting for hours."

Phonecia snorts as she places the breakfast tray on the table by the window. "Oh, go on, Miss Stanley. It's eight thirty. Same time I bring your breakfast every morning."

"Well, at least I see you wore your uniform today."

Phonecia tightens her lips but holds her tongue. She wears the stupid uniform everyday, and everyday Grace says the same thing. Phonecia's not sure if it's senility or just plain nastiness.

Grace moans—some of it's gotta be faking—as she cranks her arms into the sleeves of her penoir. It's a misty rose silk with insets of yellowed lace. Lorda mercy, it must be as old as the house itself. Phonecia has tried to talk Grace into replacing it with one of them nice soft terry robes, but would Grace listen? Stubborn old bird. Phonecia hands Grace her cane and together the two hobble over to the breakfast table.

Phonecia raises the window so that King George can escape to the roof and attend to business. She glances at the sun shining through the leaves of the elm. "Gonna be a nice day."

"Hmmph," Grace grasps the arms of the Queen Anne chair and slowly lowers herself down. She lifts the silver lid on the tray to reveal, a flowered blue china bowl filled with dry cereal. "Raisen bran again?" she barks. Her mouth droops. "Take it back, and bring me some eggs."

"Now, Miss Stanley, you know we been having trouble with your bowels."

"We?" Grace pours milk from a tiny silver pitcher. Her head snaps up. "And where's my Scotch?"

"Glory be, Miss Stanley. It ain't but nine in the morning." Chuckling, Phonecia shuffles across the room to the T.V., one of the few modern conveniences Grace has allowed. "Days Of Our Lives," Grace's favorite, Phonecia's too, is about to start. Phonecia returns to the window and takes a seat opposite Grace. She stretches her legs and sighs. "Wonder what Serena's gonna do 'bout Dr. John today."

King George jumps back in the window and from there up onto Grace's lap. She strokes him as she munches her cereal, her eyes focused on the television set where Serena is sobbing after learning the truth about her husband.

Phonecia slaps her knee. "Cheating. I knew it."

Grace pipes up. "Throw him down the elevator shaft. That's what I'd do."

Phonecia rolls her eyes heavenward. Not this again. She glances across the room to where a Chippendale bureau sits in front of the door to the old Otis lift. Lately Grace has been claiming that she pushed her husbands—all four of them, mind you—down the elevator shaft. Phonecia wonders if it's alcohol or just plain senility talking. Grace should probably see a doctor, and Phonecia's tried to get her to go, but Grace won't hear of it.

"You don't believe me." Grace sticks out her chin. "But it's true." She lifts her cane and points. "You look down that shaft over there. You'll see their bones."

Phonecia chuckles and shakes her head. "You ain't never even been married Miss Stanley."

"Oh, yes, Smartie?" Grace stabs the air with her cane. "Well, just go look."

Phonecia groans as she rises to her feet. "Fine." She levels Grace with a stern gaze. "But if there's nothing down there, can this be the end of it?"

Grace tightens her lips and glares back, saying nothing.

Phonecia first tries pushing the bureau. Then she puts her back into it. Squeaking in complaint the antique furniture moves a few inches. After a lot of huffing and puffing it finally clears the door. Phonecia opens it and peers down into the darkness. "I don't see no bones."

A tap on her backside nearly sends her over the threshold. She screams and throws up her arms. Staggering backwards, she recovers her balance and turns to see Grace standing right behind her. Grace gives her a sweet smile and lowers her cane. "See. That's how I did it. Easy as pie."

"Well you darn near sent me to meet my maker. Lorda mercy—"

Brrrrng. Brrrrng. Even coming from three stories below the ring of the doorbell is jarring.

"Now who could that be?" Last visitor was eight months ago, the man from the gas company telling them they needed to replace their meter. Phonecia waddles over to the window. "Bet it's those kids again." She peers down. "They love to ring the doorbell and hide." She heard a bunch of them whispering behind the hedge the other day. They think the mansion's haunted and that Grace's a ghost. Phonecia scans the dead scrub growing along the edge of the house. "Don't see no one." *Brrrrng. Brrrrng.* She sighs and straightens "Best go on down and see who it is." The doorbell continues to hound her as she slowly makes her way downstairs. "Coming," she shouts.

An adult figure darkens the leaded glass door. Phonecia glances down at her white uniform, calculating whether there's time for her to run and change. *Brrrrng. Brrrrng.* There's not. With a deep sigh she opens the door.

Standing on the threshold is a man, Phonecia would estimate to be in his early seventies, stocky, thick around the middle, bald on top. He's wearing one of those flowery Hawaiian shirts and a pair of rubber sandals. Beside him on the steps is a large brown duffle. He looks Phonecia up and down, obviously taking in the white uniform. She feels the heat rise to her face. "Can I help you?"

"I'm Richard Stanley. I'm here to see my sister, Grace."

* * *

Phonecia watches Grace's face as Grace stares at the figure standing in her bedroom doorway. The flowered shirt, them rubber sandals... He sure don't look like anyone fit to be Grace's brother.

"Who're you?" Grace barks.

"Richard." His smile is more of a smirk.

Grace frowns.

He steps into the room. "Richard Stanley. Your brother. Remember?" Something about his jowls reminds Phonecia of a bull dog.

Grace's face clears. "Dickie?"

"I go by Richard now."

Brother and sister face each other, staring, silent. Richard glances over at the peeling wall paper. "I see you've let the place run down."

Grace tightens her lips. "When did they let you out of jail?" Phonecia seems to remember something about Grace's brother having legal troubles, something to do with his business and gambling and people's money.

A muscle in Richard's jaw twitches. "It wasn't jail, Grace. It was the state correctional facility in Lompoc. Totally different—"

Grace snorts. "You always were a bad seed."

Wasn't there something about Grace's brother having been adopted? The way the two are glaring at each other Phonecia'd never guess they were family. She points toward the window. "Why don't you all have a seat?" They just stare at her. "Uh, maybe I could bring some tea?" No one moves. It's as if they didn't hear a word she said.

"What'n hell are you doing here?" Grace asks her brother.

He makes a sweeping gesture. "This is my home, Gracie. I've come back here to live."

*   *   *

Two weeks later…

"Days Of Our Lives" is on T.V. but neither Phonecia nor Grace are paying any attention. Grace glances toward the bedroom door and leans toward Phonecia. "He says he's going to turn this place into a museum. Says I have to move out."

There's a pleading in Grace's eyes that tugs at Phonecia's heart. "Well, I certainly hope you told him *no*," she says.

Grace sits up straight. "I most certainly did."

Phonecia smiles to see the fire back in Grace's eyes. "That's good, Miss Stanley. That's good." She nods with force. "Never want to let a bully have his way. Otherwise you in trouble for sure." Phonecia gazes out the window and frowns. She hasn't told Grace yet, but she's more than a little disturbed by the phone conversation she overheard yesterday. She'd changed out of her uniform and was about to slip out the back door when something stopped her. Down the hall in the den Richard was talking on the phone. Phonecia'd never been known to be nosy. All the same she couldn't help overhearing—something about what would happen if Grace dies, and would him be heir to the Stanley estate. Why, the very thought of that low-life getting Miss Stanley's money. Him in his rubber sandals and flowered shirt. No gentleman dresses like that...

Phonecia's so deep in thought, she fails to notice the figure in the doorway.

"Good morning, ladies."

The man didn't even have the manners to knock. His paunch bulges underneath one of them knit golf shirts. Phonecia takes in his smirk and feels her hackles rise.

He plants his eyes on his sister. "Grace." He smiles like a preacher bearing the good news. "We've come up with a new plan. You can stay right here. However, you." He turns to Phonecia. "Your services will no longer be needed."

Phonecia feels her jaw drop. She looks from Richard to Grace and back again. "You mean I'm let go?"

Richard smiles. "That's right."

Grace glares at her brother. "How dare you. You have no right to fire my maid."

Phonecia's so het up she doesn't even mind being called a maid.

Richard laughs but it comes out more like a cackle. "I have every right. I've spoken to attorneys." He takes a step toward Phonecia. "I want you out of here within the hour." There's something about the steel in his eyes that sends a chill through her gut.

The minute he's gone, Grace turns to Phonecia, her eyes glistening. "What shall I do without you?" She covers her face and begins to whimper.

Phonecia pats Grace's shoulder. "Now, now. Everything gonna be all right." She wishes she believed that herself.

Grace dabs at her eyes. "You think he really is entitled to this house? Mother was the last to die and she failed to make a will and—"

Phonecia shakes her head. "All I know, Miss Stanley, is that that man is no good."

"What shall I do?" Grace asks.

Phonecia glances across the room and strokes her chin. "Let me think on this."

*　　　*　　　*

The next morning finds Grace and Phonecia sitting in their same chairs by the third story bedroom window, waiting for the next episode of "Days Of Our Lives." Across the room King George sniffs the door to the elevator shaft, his tail twitching.

"You think Serena'll divorce Dr. John today?" Phonecia asks Grace.

"Bring me a scotch," she barks.

Slowly Phonecia gets up and harrumphs her way down the hall to the bathroom. She returns with a glass half full of amber liquid and sets it down on the table with a firm clunk, but she doesn't take her seat. Instead she goes over and turns off the T.V.

"What'd you do that for?" Grace squawks.

Phonecia plants herself squarely in front of Grace. "Now listen, Miss Stanley. Given as all that's gone on around here lately, and given as I saved your goose..." She fingers her white uniform. "Don't you think it's time I started wearing regular clothes?"

Grace glances across the room at the giant bottle of Chlorox sitting by the door to the elevator shaft. She looks at Phonecia. "Well, maybe you're right."

"Thank you." Phonecia returns to the television and switches it back on. On her way back she stops by the elevator shaft, opens the door, and pours in a good glunk-glunk of the Chlorox. She shuts the door and returns to sit by Grace.

On T.V. Serena sobs into a Kleenex.

Grace turns to Phonecia and smiles. "And why don't you stop calling me *Miss Stanley*. Sounds too formal. *Grace* will do just fine."

Fish Angel
for Gwendolyn & Charlotte

It was a night late in August, and the desert blew its hot winds over the land toward the sea. Grandmother Gloria propelled herself in her ancient cane wheelchair to the door of the hut where she could look out. "Children, come see," she exclaimed. "*Mira.* Look. The stars are falling."

Seven-year-old Herminia, her dark eyes round as seashells, stood beside her grandmother gazing out at the starlight. "What does it mean, *Abuelita?*"

Her *abuela* smiled. "God is having a soccer game, *mija.* The angels are kicking the stars across the sky. See?" She pointed.

Ten-year-old Carlito blew air through his lips and laughed silently. Did his grandmother really expect them to believe this stuff?

Grandmother Gloria patted Herminia's arm. "Hurry, child. Grab a basket and run catch some stars."

Carlito stood beside his grandmother and watched as his little sister raced from the hut with her basket, crossed the dirt road, and scampered over the sea wall onto the beach. He looked down at his grandmother. The skin on her arms reminded him of the yellow mud that comes when it rains and then dries and cracks in the sun. "What are you waiting for, child?" she asked him. "Go have fun."

He shrugged and picked up his bucket. "Maybe I'll dig for clams." When he reached the beach, he caught sight of his sister far down along the shoreline, skipping at the water's edge. Her braids flew out behind her. Her feet barely touched the sand. In one hand she swung her basket. With the other she reached for the stars.

Carlito was used to the brilliant night skies on the Sea of Cortez, where a serape of stars spread across the heavens, and the light was so bright you could see your own shadow. But never before had he seen a night like this. Streaks of fire shot from horizon to horizon. Tiny balls of light fell from the sky.

Out on the ocean rows of waves rumbled in, their froth an iridescent, white-green glow. Suddenly, a giant ball of fire the size of a donkey cart came crackling down from the sky. It plunged straight into the ocean, sending up a fan of silvery spray. Carlito dropped to the sand and covered his head.

Herminia streaked up the beach to join him. Waves raced into shore. The two children ran for the shelter of their hut.

Herminia told her grandmother, "The sky is falling."

Grandmother Gloria smiled. "The angels are having fun."

*   *   *

The next morning the sea had pulled itself back like a bed sheet, exposing miles and miles of wet sand. Carlito rose while his sister and grandmother still lay sleeping and went down to the beach. Above him the sky was painted its normal bright blue, not a sign of the fire show of the night before. He crossed the narrow boardwalk that the fisherman had built to trailer their dories down to the ocean. On Sundays Grandmother Gloria traveled down this same wooden path in her wheelchair to watch the pelicans dive into the sea. The early morning breeze from the south brought with it a strange, soft moaning. Carlito, busy digging for clams, straightened and listened. *Nada.* He stooped to go after another clam and heard it again. "*Ayudame. Ayuuuudame.*"

Ayuda? Was someone crying for help? Then Carlito saw it—a huge dark, glistening blob lying in the wet sand right near the high tide mark. He hurried closer. Was it a baby whale? Sometimes whales beached themselves and died, and then there was a mighty stink that floated around the village for weeks. When Carlito got within a few yards of the creature,

39

he noticed its silvery scales and its fins. *Díos mío!* It was an enormous fish, and it was caught in a net.

"*Ayuuudame.*" Its rubbery lips formed a giant smooch as it made the "*yuuu*" sound.

Carlito crept closer.

The creature eyed him through the net. "*Buenos dias.*"

Carlito jerked backwards and almost sat down. "You can speak?"

"*Claro que sí.*" Its voice was low and gravelly and sounded like Tio Stefano, the village drunk. "I am an angel," the creature declared.

Carlito leaned closer. "*Un angel?*"

"*Sí.* I fell from the sky into the sea." Another moan.

Carlito remembered the giant ball of fire of the night before.

"Do you know what it's like to hit the water going the speed of light?" the creature asked.

Carlito shook his head.

The fish lowered its eyelids. "Well, I assure you, it does not feel good. Friction damned near burned my feathers off."

Carlito eyed the fish suspiciously. "An angel of God would not curse."

The fish's eyelids snapped up. "Oh, yeah? How do you think you'd like it if your feathers were on fire?"

Carlito noticed what look like the charred ends of pinions sticking out from among the creature's scales. He also noticed that its fins had joints. They did look a lot more like wings than fish fins. He took in the rolls of blubber that hung from the fish's body, the droopy jowls, the scaly eyebrows, the little prickly things on its face that could have been angel feathers but looked more like whiskers. "I've never heard of an angel that was a fish before. There's nothing about it in the Bible."

The fish rolled its eyes. "The Bible isn't everything." It took in a deep breath and blew out a fine mist. "So, *escucha, chico*. I need help. You gotta get me out of this fishnet and back into the water." It flapped its useless wing-fins.

Carlito reached for the net and gave it a big tug. It wouldn't budge. With a sigh he straightened. The creature must have weighed at least as much as their neighbor Jose's burro. "I'll be back," he told the fish. He scampered up the beach to the hut to get a knife. When he returned, the mayor Raul Rodriguez, Father Miguel, the priest, and Jaime Puentes, the owner of El Pescado, the best and only restaurant in the village, were all three standing around the fish creature. Its eyes were closed. Its black tongue lolled from the side of its mouth. It wasn't moving.

Carlito turned to Father Miguel. "This fish is an angel, Padre."

The priest's bushy eyebrows rose. "*Un angel?* What are you saying, my son?"

Carlito turned to the mayor. "It told me it fell from the sky."

The mayor burst out laughing. "A fish that can talk? Now that's a good one."

Carlito switched his gaze back to the father. "But it's true, Padre. *Mira.*" Carlito planted himself directly in front of the fish. "*Habla,*" he commanded.

The fish lay as still as stone.

Jaime Puentes folded his arms, and tilted his head. "There's enough here to feed the entire village." He stroked his chin. "First we fillet it." He circled the fish angel. "Then we add onions, garlic, plenty of jalapeño." He licked his lips. "Very tasty."

The creature's eyes flew open, but only Carlito noticed.

The three men left, Jaime Puentes declaring he would return in an hour with helpers to carve up the fish.

The minute the men were gone, the fish angel spoke up. "Did you hear that kid? They're going to fillet me alive."

Carlito put his fists on his hips. "Well, then why didn't you tell them you're an angel?"

"Third rule in The Commandments for Angels, my son. Once thou hast spoken to one human, thou must speak to no other."

The sun had climbed higher in the sky. Steam rose from the creature's flesh. An unmistakably fishy odor filled the air.

"Do me a favor, kid," the angel fish said. "Put a little water on my back."

Carlito ran with his bucket down to the sea, returned, and doused the fish.

A soft swish of breath escaped its gills. "Gracias, kid. I needed that."

Carlito used his knife to free the creature from the net. Next he tried to roll it toward the water. He got it halfway over on its side, but then it rolled right back again. "Ow," it howled. "You got sand in my eyes." It scrunched up its scaly eyebrows. "Man, that burns worse than fairy dust." Carlito asked it to try flopping forward while he pushed. They made it a few feet doing that, but then the fish angel began to complain that he was going to have a heart attack if they kept it up. Carlito rose to his feet. He gazed out at the ocean. The tide was still far, far out.

"I'll be back," he told the fish. He returned to the hut and explained the situation to his grandmother.

"Save an angel?" she exclaimed. "Why, darling, you must."

Carlito stared at his grandmother. "But how?"

"I'm not quite sure." His grandmother folded her hands and closed her eyes. She opened them again. "Just, maybe, this might work…"

A few minutes later Carlito and his little sister Herminia could be seen pushing their grandmother's empty chair, down the boardwalk to the sea. To Carlito's relief the fish angel was still there on the beach lying exactly where he'd left it. They rolled the wheelchair off the boardwalk onto the sand and dragged it over to the fish. They turned the chair on its side and pushed it up as close to the sea creature as they possibly could. With rope from the hut they tethered the enormous fish to the chair. Next they attached a line to one of the wooden arms. Backing away for a distance, as their grandmother had instructed, they began to tug. They strained and huffed, but the chair wouldn't budge.

"Go get help," Carlito instructed Herminia.

Herminia raced back to the hut. "*Abuelita,*" she wailed, "we are not strong enough."

The grandmother sat silent for a moment, her sagging eyes searching for answers. She raised a crooked finger. "*Ya lo tengo.*" I have it.

Two minutes later Herminia returned to the beach. In one hand she held the rein of Florita, the neighbor's burro. In the other, she dangled a carrot, just out of reach. Proceeding in this manner, the two crossed the sand to the spot where Carlito stood guard. The burro lowered its head and sniffed at the blubbery blob.

"Get that thing away from me," wailed the fish.

"This burro is going to save your life," Carlito informed the creature. He tied the burro's rein to the rope that was attached to the arm of the wheelchair. Using the carrot as enticement, he encouraged the burro to begin pulling. The wicker of the antique wheelchair squeaked in protest. The fish angel groaned and complained that his tethers were too tight. Popping sounds could be heard as the back of the chair began to tear from its frame. Slowly, painfully, the chair rose up off the sand and back onto its wheels, fish angel and all.

Now in normal powdery sand it would have been impossible to push the wheelchair with that big fat fish in it even an inch. But, fortunately, the sun had dried the wet sand to the perfect hardness. Mixed with a little angel dust, it made a solid surface on which the wheelchair might move.

The sound of deep voices rose above the distant roar of the ocean. A group of men headed up the beach their way. It was Jaime Puentes and his helpers from the restaurant. Their machetes gleamed in the sunlight.

"Yikes," shrieked the fish. "They're coming to filet me."

With the help of the burro the two children managed to get the wheelchair up onto the boardwalk. Quickly Carlito removed the tethers holding the creature to the chair, then he and his sister began pushing it toward the sea. Shuddering, squeaking, rattling, the rickety old wheelchair gradually gathered speed. By the time it neared the end of the boardwalk, it was going almost faster than the two children could run.

"Yippee," shouted the fish, its whiskers flattened against its face by the wind.

The children held tight to the wheelchair's handles and counted to three. Abruptly they stopped, jerking the chair backwards. The momentum sent the fish angel flying. "Glory hallelujah," it shouted as it soared through the air. With a very large splash it landed in the ocean. The last they saw of it was its tail as it dove for deeper waters.

That night the stars again tumbled from the sky, and this time they fell all the way to earth. Covering the wet sand were millions and millions of round white discs. If you looked at them closely you could see the outline of an angel right in their centers. Herminia gathered them in her basket. Carlito used his bucket. They took the fallen stars home to the grandmother. She made pretty jewelry out of them which Carlito sold at the market. They used the money to buy Grandmother Gloria a new wheelchair.

The Purple Madonna

On the coast of Mexico, approximately a hundred miles south of Acapulco, lies the sleepy little village of Azucán. Tucked into a tropical hillside, it overlooks the Bay of Los Tres Santos. In the year of our Lord nineteen hundred and fifty-eight, pigs still roam its back alleys. Women wash their laundry in the Rio De Las Rosas. Occasionally a yacht heading north from Panama will anchor in its bay, but, unlike its bustling neighbor to the north, Azucán has not yet experienced the abundance nor the corruption brought on by American tourism. There is one church, *La Iglesia De Las Rosas*, and its priest is *el Padre Diego de Obregón*.

* * *

The afternoon sun has dropped halfway towards its resting place in the sea when Padre Diego limps toward the confessional. With a sigh and a pulling-in of his gut, he squeezes through the narrow doorway. Grunting, he slowly lowers himself down onto the hard, wooden bench. His feet are so swollen he can barely buckle his sandals. His ankles throb. Stop eating Pepito's tamales, the doctor tells him. *Díos mío.* How could anyone do that? If only he could put his feet up, but that's impossible in the cramped space of the confessional. *Dos horas.* Two hours he'll have to be cooped up like this. He sighs and inwardly prays for strength.

The clop of leather soles on tile approaches. The entry door to the confessional squeaks open. A cloud of spicy cologne drifts through the hole in the wall that separates sinner from priest. Don Jorge is that sinner. Father Diego'd know the scent of his aftershave anywhere. The father shifts his weight slightly and waits for what he knows is coming.

Perdóname Padre porque he pecado. "Forgive me, Father, for I have sinned." Silence. "Father, I have committed a sin against my marriage…" Adultery. It's the same every week. Don Jorge just can't seem to stay away from Conchita down at the town square, nor can any of the other men of the village for that matter. Conchita makes a killing, and Father Diego makes sure she donates plenty of it to the church. He assigns Don Jorge twelve Hail Marys and orders him to leave and sin no more. Not likely.

Two and a half hours later Father Diego emerges from the confessional, exhausted. He thought Elena Gonzalez would never stop talking. Instead of relaying her own sins, she went on and on about the transgressions of others. Far more troubling, though, was Adolfo Morillo's story. Adolfo had been hoping to be promoted to head clerk at the bank, but instead his neighbor Miguel, who'd been spreading false rumors about Adolfo, got the position and Adolfo got fired. Father Diego cringes as he recalls the venom in Adolfo's words. Adolfo wants retribution. Miguel should be warned, but the seal of the confessional prohibits Father Diego from saying or doing anything. He sighs. He must leave it in God's hands.

From high above the altar Our Blessed Virgin sheds her benevolent gaze upon the good father. He genuflects, turns, and limps slowly down the center aisle. If his feet get much worse, he may have to start using a cane like *un viejo*. *Por favor, Díos*, no. Emerging from the dark tranquility of the church he pauses on the steps where he can look down over his village. The sun, not far from setting, glares off the sea. Street noises surround him—a taxi honking, a truck banging its way down the cobblestone street, dogs barking. From inside the walled garden on the corner comes the sound of children at play. He catches a whiff of leather emanating from the saddle store across the street. A cart selling tacos sends up aromas that could make a sinner out of a saint. Father Diego's stomach growls. What he needs is one of Pepito's tamales. The question is can he make it all the way to the plaza on foot? He begins limping down the sidewalk in that direction. A taxi screeches to a stop on the cobblestones below him and his friend Carlos leans out. "Give you a ride, Father?"

Father Diego lifts his eyes heavenward and mouths a silent prayer of thanks.

*   *   *

The strings of light bulbs hanging from posts surrounding the town square are just coming on when Father Diego sits down on a bench to enjoy his tamales and beer. It's Saturday night, a popular time for the young people of the pueblo to stroll around the *zócalo*. Teenage girls walk arm in arm, carefully watched by chaperones following closely behind. Some of the girls are already wearing their fiesta dresses. The feast of our Blessed Virgin of Guadalupe is only a week away. Teenaged boys, dressed in black pants and white shirts, circle the plaza in the opposite direction. Each time one winks or smiles at a girl, he gets a severe look from her *dueña*. As they pass by Father Diego, each nods, and he nods back. He knows them all by name. In fact, he knows every single soul in the entire village—his flock. It's his job to guard them.

Fourteen-year-old Catalina Sanchez locks eyes with sixteen-year-old Lepe Torres as the two pass. They are sweethearts, and judging from the confessions Father Diego's been hearing from Catalina, things have already gone too far. With twelve children what the Sanchez family does not need is another mouth to feed. Father Diego will talk to Señora Sanchez. He will say, "Your daughter Catalina is very beautiful. You must keep a watchful eye." He can say this without breaking the seal of the confessional. Señora Sanchez will know exactly what he means. They all do. He sighs. If only he could solve the Adopho Morillo situation so easily.

Across the square Father Diego catches a glimpse of Don Jorge descending the stairway from Conchita Muñoz's apartment. And to think only an hour ago Don Jorge was sitting in his confessional. Father Diego sighs. Abruptly Don Jorge turns a corner and disappears down the alley. A few minutes later Conchita herself appears. She cradles her ample bosoms and makes a quick adjustment, then descends the stairs. Her lacy low-cut blouse is Oaxacan as is her brightly embroidered, flowered skirt. At the bottom of the stairs, she plucks a red hibiscus from a bush and sticks it behind her ear. She crosses the plaza and smiles when she sees Father Diego.

"*Muy buenos noches*, Padre." Each cheek is a circle of red rouge, and there are tiny cracks in the powdery face makeup she wears, but, oh, those eyes, limpid pools of dark brown. Is it any wonder the men of the village have so much trouble resisting her? "I am going for to get some of Pepito's tamales." She eyes the corn husk wrappings on his lap. "Would you like me to bring you some, Father?"

The padre wipes the grease from his chin with a tiny napkin. He blushes and smiles. "I couldn't."

Conchita smiles back showing her dimples. "Oh, Padre. I'll bet you could." She goes and within minutes returns with four tamales wrapped in yellow paper. She takes a seat on the bench beside Father Diego and offers him one.

The aroma of the tamales may be captivating, but the flowery scent emanating from Conchita is even more so. Father Diego avoids glancing at her silky breasts. Ay, Conchita. Like swollen ankles, she is another of his crosses to bear.

He dabs his mouth with a napkin and clears his throat. "You know, Conchita, the roof of the church has begun to leak, and we hardly have enough to fix—"

She taps his knee. "I make my donation after I go to the bank *en la mañana*." She glances at her wristwatch and rises to her feet. "Time for business. I must go."

Father Diego is just licking the remains of the last tamale from his fingertips when his old friend Manolo approaches. Manolo has ears that protrude from his head like the wings of *la paloma* and deep round eyes with long thick lashes. The eyes give him the appearance of a small boy, comical in a man of near fifty. He wears a pair of shabby tan pants and a white shirt, the sleeves rolled up to the elbows. Both shirt and pants are speckled in a variety of colored paints. Father Diego gestures, and Manolo takes a seat. "*Cómo se va?*" Father Diego asks him.

"*Bien. Bien.*" Manolo, who is the official town carpenter, painter, artist, and man of all trades, tells Father Diego of a very fortuitous event that has just come to pass. Manolo's uncle, who lives in the village on the other side of the mountain, died. Of course, that, in itself, is not the good news, but what is, is that the uncle bequeathed his burro to Manolo. Like so many of the men of the village, responsible for supporting their large Catholic broods, Manolo does not own a car—not that one would help him in his work. Most of the roads where he goes are too steep and narrow for a motorized vehicle. So everyday Manolo has to haul his cartload of tools and cans of paint up and down the hills of the pueblo on foot. But now, praise God, he has a burro who will pull the cart and he will ride the burro.

Father Diego raises his eyes to the heavens and makes the sign of the cross. "God has cast his blessing upon you, my son."

Manolo nods. "Indeed, he has, Father. Indeed, he has." Manolo gazes up at the evening sky and smiles. Father Diego heaves a contented sigh and stretches out his legs. He is about to take a sip of beer when he feels bristles against his cheek and a blast of warm breath against his neck. Something nudges his shoulder. All of a sudden, his bottle of beer is being wrenched from his grasp. He turns to see a burro standing right behind him. Clenched firmly between its teeth is his bottle of beer. The burro lifts its head and with a *glunk, glunk* guzzles the entire bottle-full.

Manolo leaps to his feet. "*Ay, ay, ay*, Gabino." Way too late, he grabs the burro by its dangling rein and gives it a severe yank. The burro drops the bottle on the ground and lets out a belch. It pulls back its lips so you can see its peg-shaped teeth and grins. At least that's how Father Diego would interpret the expression.

"Ay, Padre Diego," Manolo cries. "*Lo siento mucho*." I am very sorry. He explains that Gabino, his new donkey, *es muy inteligente pero es muy travieso.* He's very intelligent, but he's also very naughty. He has been trained to do things, Manolo explains. *Por ejemplo*, when Manolo is perched on a ledge, Gabino will hand him up his paint brushes. So this intelligence of the donkey is both a blessing and a curse.

Manolo ties Gabino to a nearby post. Then he goes and buys another beer for Padre Diego and one for himself. A guitarist strikes up a tune. Gentle breezes float in off the bay. It is indeed a beautiful night. The two old friends sit in silence, enjoying the evening and their companionship.

*　　*　　*

"Padre. Padre," calls a hushed voice.

Father Diego moans slightly as he turns over on his lumpy mattress. Slowly he rises to a sitting position. Out the window the sky is just beginning to gray. The roosters haven't even begun to crow yet. Who could possibly want him at this early hour? Has Rosa Puente's baby come too soon? Is ninety-year-old Señora Gutierez heaving her last breath? Stiffly he rises to his feet, dons his cassock, and limps in his bare feet across the tiles.

On the other side of the door stands Doña Marta, Don Jorge's wife. She holds a candle and wears a long white robe. Her braid which she normally wears coiled upon her head hangs over one shoulder. Her hand trembles slightly. "There's been a miracle, Padre Diego. You must come."

*   *   *

Doña Marta's ample buttocks sway from side to side like a sack full of gourds. Padre Diego climbs the steep sidewalk behind her, his huaraches squeaking in protest on his swollen feet. The sun has just made its appearance from behind the mountain and casts its golden light on the brightly painted trim of the white stucco buildings. A cock crows. A dog barks. A baby cries. Someone tosses a bucketful of gray water out a door onto the sidewalk.

Doña Marta and Padre Diego are both panting by the time they reach Doña Marta and Don Jorge's house on the corner of Calle Barco Del Mar and Avenida Santa María. Don Jorge opens the gate and greets them. Father Diego steps inside. Don Jorge points at what appears to be a nest of reddish-brown scribbles defacing the whitewashed wall just inside his gate. Padre Diego stares at the image. At first he sees nothing. He moves to the right. He moves to the left. He takes a step back. Suddenly he understands what Doña Marta has been exclaiming about—the slightly tilted head, the drape of the fabric covering it, the soft eyes, the sad-sweet smile. You have to squint, but with a little imagination and plenty of faith, it's there. You'll see it.

"*Ah, sí, sí.*" He makes the sign of the cross.

Un milagro? Maybe.

The next day it's María Sanchez who awakens him. They too have a miracle. It's on their garden wall. This time the image is yellow.

*   *   *

Two weeks have passed and four images of the virgin have been sighted. The villagers can talk of nothing else. Father Diego spoke of the miracles in his sermon on the day of the Feast of the Virgin of Guadalupe. Miracles are good for a village and he knows it.

He is sitting peacefully on a bench in the shade of a flame tree contemplating these very miracles when his friend Manolo appears. Manolo ties his donkey's rein around the trunk of the tree and takes a seat beside Father Diego.

"I have something important to tell you, Father." He lowers his voice. "I know what's behind the images people have found."

Father Diego turns his head. "You do?"

Manolo nods at his donkey. "It's Gabino."

Father Diego's jaw drops. "What?"

Manolo rises to his feet. "It's no miracle, Father." He goes over to his donkey. "Gabino likes to cool his tail in the open cans of paint." He lifts the donkey's tail. Sure enough, there are remnants of green paint on the bristles. "I've been doing work at each of the *casas* where these images have occurred. I'm afraid it is my donkey who is the artist, not God.

"Shhh." Father Diego madly pounds the air. "You must remove the paint from the donkey's tail immediately, Manolo. You must tell no one."

"But, Father—"

"*Silencio.*" Father Diego inserts a sternness into his voice. "Now you listen to me, Manolo. Because of the image on his wall Don Jorge has stopped visiting Conchita. He delivers flowers to his wife every night, and you know the Sanchez family? I've been worried sick that their daughter Catalina will become pregnant by Lepe Torres, but, since seeing the image on her garden wall, Catalina Sanchez has decided to join a nunnery. Best of all, Adolpho Morillo and his neighbor Manuel have mended their friendship. People have only to believe in miracles, Manolo, and they will happen."

Manolo nods. "I see, Father. Indeed, I see."

*   *   *

It's the eve of the birth of our Savior. Manolo has just delivered a large box of votive candles to the church and is helping the good father lay them out.

Manolo winks. "Any more miracles to report, Father?"

"Very funny." Father Diego gestures toward a bench. "Let's sit down a minute. I'm exhausted." He limps over and slowly lowers himself onto the hard wooden surface. Ay, the miracles. The miracles. Since Don Jorge stopped cheating on his wife, the rest of the men of the village have reformed as well. They no longer visit Conchita. For their wives this is a blessing, but for Conchita it is a curse. She's going broke. Padre Diego sighs. And she used to be one of his biggest donors.

Manolo nods at the father's feet which are so red and swollen they look like they might explode. "Pepito's tamales?"

Father Diego shakes his head. "No. The doctor said that's what it was, but it can't be because Pepito just retired. He's closed the tamale shop. I haven't had one of his tamales in a week." Father Diego drops his head. The sun might as well not shine, nor the moon come up, if he can't enjoy Pepito's tamales.

*   *   *

On Christmas day Father Diego rises just as the cock crows. He dons his white gown in honor of the nativity and around his neck he hangs a Christmas stole of white silk embroidered with golden doves. He's in the process of lighting the candles inside the church, when a ray of morning sunshine floods through the open side door illuminating an alcove along the west wall of the church. Something high up catches the priest's eye, colors that were never there before. He blinks and moves closer. It looks a little like the images painted by the donkey's tail on the villagers' walls only this is different. He gasps and steps back. Why, it's a purple Madonna, and it covers almost the entire wall of the alcove. With her eyes cast down, she's so beautiful. Surrounding her head are masses of colored flowers—roses, an allusion to the miracle of Guadalupe, Father Diego has no doubt. He stares and stares, unable to take his eyes away. Could Manolo's donkey possibly have been responsible for this? As if his thoughts had wings…

"Feliz Navidad, Padre." It's Manolo. Father Diego was so enraptured by the purple Madonna, that he didn't even hear his friend come in.

Father Diego points at the wall. "*Por favor*, Manolo, explain to me how your donkey did this."

Manolo gazes up at the wall. "Why, Father, my donkey could never have done such a thing. To begin with it's too high on the wall, and even though I will admit the animal is an artist, he's quite incapable of producing a creation like this."

Father Diego eyes his friend with suspicion. Manolo wouldn't lie, would he? Certainly not to a priest and not on the day of our Savior's birth.

*   *   *

Christmas mass fills Father Diego with more rapture than he ever remembers experiencing. Every so often during the service, he glances up at the purple Madonna, and each time he does he is filled with an inexplicable joy. It isn't until after mass when he is standing outside the church sharing Christmas greetings with his flock that he realizes something else has changed. His feet have stopped hurting. When no one is looking, surreptitiously he lifts his gown. Why, praise to God, his feet and ankles have shrunk to normal size. Could it be the purple Madonna? He's just pondering that question when Conchita Muñoz rushes up. "Father, I have wonderful news." She's wearing a blouse with a chaste lace collar instead of one of her low-cut ones. "Pepito shared his recipe for the tamales with me. I'm going to take over his shop."

Father Diego smiles and raises his eyes heavenward. Will miracles never cease?

*   *   *

Was the purple Madonna on the wall of *La Iglesia de las Rosas* God's work or done by the hand of man? The way Manolo saw it, it made no difference. In Father Diego's own words, "People have only to believe in miracles, and they will happen." Manolo got rid of the evidence. On the day after Christmas in the year of our Lord nineteen hundred and fifty-eight, he and his donkey hiked upriver about a mile above town. There Manolo dumped the remainder of a gallon full of purple paint into the Río De Las Rosas. Only the frigate birds, circling high on the wind drafts above Azucán, saw him do it. The paint turned the waters of the río purple. Downstream the village women doing their laundry noticed their fabrics turning a most becoming shade of lavender. Praise God. It is another miracle.

The UFO Motel

There's a stretch of desert somewhere east of Roswell, New Mexico that claims more UFO sightings than any place else on earth, and that's why Lucy and Lew Laredo opened a motel there. Out in the middle of nowhere, alongside Interstate 70 west, a billboard rises out of the landscape. "UFO Hunts," it says. "Over 1000 Sightings A Year, NO HOAXES." Below that it offers a10% Discount if you stay at the motel.

On the wall in the motel lobby next to the framed membership certificate from MUFON—that's Mutual UFO Network—and a picture of a Flying Purple People Eater, hangs a faded and fuzzy photo of Lew Laredo standing in the desert. Floating above his head is a silvery disk, the very same saucer that landed back in 1971. As the story goes, a door opened, a ladder dropped down, and three little men in white suits got out. It wasn't the rapture that took Grandma. No, siree. It was the little men from outer space. The event became inspiration for country western singer Chet Hawkin's number one hit, "The Day Granny Got Kidnapped by the UFO." Lew and Lucy saw the whole thing with their very own eyes, and for only twenty-five dollars you can see it too. Well, maybe not the same flying saucer, but you'll see at least one UFO, guaranteed or your money back.

NO HOAXES.

*   *   *

Lew's deep into the centerfold of the February issue of Playboy when the bell above the lobby door jingles. Quickly he flips the magazine over and plants a smile on his face. Could be a customer. It's not. It's Cousin Larry, a plumber's friend dripping water on the lobby rug in his hand. Lew's smile droops.

Larry raises the rubber tool. "Them dang tampons. Stop up a toilet every time." As always, he's wearing a pair of stained Levis and a dirty white T shirt with the sleeves cutoff. His tattooed biceps are the size of ham hocks. He reaches for the Playboy and grins. "How'd you like Miss February?"

Lew snatches the magazine back and shoves it under the counter. "I only read the jokes."

"Yeah, right."

The bell above the door jingles again. This time it *is* customers. A family of four. Cousin Larry slips past them and out the door. Lew's all smiles. "Afternoon, folks."

The woman says, "hello," but the man just nods. One of the boys, a kid about eight, glances at his mother then at Lew. "You really have UFOs around here?"

"Yes siree, son. That we do." Lew points at the wall. "There's a picture of one right over there." The boy's father is already examining the MUFON certificate that hangs beside the photo of Lew and the saucer.

The kid's older brother pipes up. "Dad says this is all a big hoax."

"Trevor." His mother grabs him by the shoulders and claps her hand over his mouth. She smiles at Lew and shrugs. "Sorry."

Lew's grin is as wide as the Bandera Crater. "No problem, ma'am." He winks. "Got a grandson about his age." He nods at a photo on the wall behind him.

The mother leans over the counter, squints, then smiles. "Oh, isn't he cute."

The kid's dad saunters back and begins thumbing through the stack of pamphlets on the counter. Along with a copy of the current MUFON journal, there are leaflets advertising Barking

Sands, others for the Petrified Forest, and the dinosaur caves on Interstate 10. Lew gets these materials free from the Auto Club. Figures advertising other roadside attractions makes his business seem a little more authentic.

The dad eyes Lew. "So is this UFO thing legit?" He pronounces it, "You-fo." Larry always does that too. They're not *youfos*. They're *U F O's*. Lew picks up a copy of the recent MUFON journal and hands it to the man. "Ever heard of UFOLOGY?" he asks.

The man scratches his head. "Can't say I have."

"It's the study of UFOs," Lew tells him. "You can read all about it right here."

"What's MUFON?" the man asks. He pronounces it "muff-on," which triggers a vision of the Playboy centerfold that Lew's been trying to repress.

"Stands for Mutual UFO Network," Lew explains. "It was started back in 1969."

The man strokes his soul patch as he studies the MUFON journal. Lew refrains from mentioning Grandma. You don't want to push it too far with these skeptical types.

The eight-year-old tugs at his dad's arm. "Can we see the UFOs, dad. Please? Please?" Now *he* pronounces UFO correctly. His mother fingers the stack of T-shirts advertising the motel.

Lew did the designs himself. Hell, they've even got green aliens on the front just like the shirts they sell over at the Roswell Museum.

The man drops the journal and levels Lew with a gaze. "So are you telling me you can predict these things?"

"Oh, no." Lew widens his eyes. "I don't pretend to predict a thing." He points at the money-back guarantee sign. "That's why you'll get your money back if they don't come." He rests his arms on the counter and leans toward the man. "But I'll tell you something." He lowers his voice and looks around like it's some kinda big secret. "There've been solar flares lately. Almost sure to be a UFO sighting after a flare."

The man looks at his wife. She shrugs. He shakes his head at Lew. "I don't think so."

"Aw, Dad," the eight-year-old squawks.

"Scam," his dad mutters.

*   *   *

Lew and Lucy's flatbed rears and bucks as it negotiates an especially tight curve. Flash floods a few weeks earlier have made potholes in the desert that go all the way to China. Ten guests from the UFO Motel sit on benches in the back, holding onto the railings for dear life.

When they go on a UFO hunt, Cousin Larry goes out first in the jeep. At Dead Man's Bluff he veers left and parks his vehicle where it won't be seen. He carries his equipment and climbs the bluff on foot, then, like an outlaw about to ambush a stagecoach, he crouches and waits for the arrival of the sightseers. Once they're beyond him and down in the valley, he sets the balloons off. Wind's gotta be just right, but usually it's pretty dependable. Blows west to east. Sends them babies floating right off over the valley where all those sightseers are standing, waiting, hoping, praying for a glimpse of a UFO. Does Lew feel guilty about this little deception? Well, maybe just a little, but what the hell, they provide a darn good show, and anyway, once in a while—you might say once in fifty years—the real thing comes along.

Lew's gray ponytail flops against the back of his neck with each bump. Lucy sticks out her arms and braces herself against the dashboard as they negotiate another hairpin turn. She winces and frowns at her husband. "Can't you make it a little smoother? My piles are killing me."

Lew looks in his rearview mirror and grimaces at the angry faces of Mr. and Mrs. Jefferson. "Don't think the couple staying in 208 bought it, Mother."

Lucy slides her bulk over and checks in the mirror. "Whew. They look mad." She shakes her head causing her dangling jowls to swing. "Bet they're gonna ask for their money back. Just like those people did last week."

Lew cringes. They're barely able to make ends meet these days. Folks just don't seem as interested in UFOs as they used to be. All the rooms on the first floor need new plumbing and Lucy's been telling him that the sheets and towels need to be replaced. Hells bells, where're they gonna get the money?

"Them Mylar party balloons don't take the wind like the weather balloons do." Lucy says. "And they're too small. They just don't look as real."

Lew switched to Mylar because the weather balloons were going up in price, and the last time he tried to order them off his favorite website, they sent him pink. Now who'n the hell ever heard of a pink UFO? They'd look like a bunch of flying titties.

*   *   *

Sure enough, the minute they arrive back at the motel, the Jeffersons demand a refund. Then the Jacobs from cabin 109 do the same. Darn chain reaction starts, and by the time it's done, Lew's had to reimburse everyone except for the elderly couple from room 115. They loved it.

The mail is waiting on the desk in the office. Right on top is a package from Lawson's Party City in Albuquerque. Lew opens his pocket knife and guides the blade along the strip of tape on the top of the box. Inside silvery Mylar glistens from beneath mounds of plastic bubbles. Whew. At least they got the color right this time. He lifts out the stack of 32 inch balloons. "Oh shit," he cries.

Lucy swivels in her chair. "What is it, hon?"

"Look, Mother." He holds up one of the balloons. There's a canary yellow Tweety Bird right in the center.

"Oh, dear." Lucy swivels back to her desk and begins thumbing through the mail. She holds up an envelope. "Wonder what this is." She puts on her reading glasses. "It's from the Discovery Channel."

Lew draws down the sides of his mouth. "Thought we paid the cable bill."

"We did, hon. This is different." Lucy's eyes widen. "Why, I'll be." She looks at Lew over the top of her glasses. "Says they're gonna do a series, UFOs: Hoax or Real?" She removes her glasses and rises to her feet. "They want to come here." She opens her arms to Lew. "They're gonna put us on T.V."

He lets out a shout and swings her around in a do-si-do—not an easy feat, given she weighs over two hundred pounds, and he's a scrawny hundred and forty. He steps back. His eyes lock with hers. "We're gonna have to do a lot better than them dang party balloons."

*   *   *

The brisk spring night couldn't be better, so clear you can see all the way to heaven and back, so bright the barrel cactus are casting shadows. Smell of sage in the air, soft breeze out of the west. Perfect for a meeting with the unknown.

The camera crew from the Discovery Channel stands in silence. No one speaks but a whisper. Everyone's heads are craned back, all eyes glued heavenward. At nine p.m. right on the dot—.

"Look." Someone points at the sky. Sure enough, from out behind Dead Man's Bluff a silver disk-shaped object has appeared. Moonshine reflects off its surface. Lights flash on and off from its underbelly. Lew and Lucy hold hands as it approaches. Hell, the thing looks pretty darned real. Sure should after what it cost. Lew got a hold of the guy who helped make the balloon for that little kid who was thought to have floated away. It was all over the news just a few years back—nothing but a hoax. Anyway, Lew paid the man nine hundred and seventy five dollars to make another weather balloon just like the one the kid used and another two hundred and fifty to affix battery driven flashing lights.

John Tapp, the producer for the Discovery Channel, holds up a mic. He steps over to Lew. "Well, well, Mr. Laredo, it looks like the show's begun."

Lew, faking awe, makes his eyes go big. "Ain't it something?" Lucy squeezes his hand.

The producer grins. "So, how'd you do it?" He shoves the mic at Lew.

Lew lets go of Lucy's hand. "How'd I do it?" His heart accelerates. "I don't know what you mean."

The interviewer laughs. "Oh, come on, Mr. Laredo. We know all about those shipments you've been getting from Party City."

The worry in Lucy's eyes makes Lew's heart ache. He fakes a chuckle. "Oh, those. Grandkids, don't you know. One of 'em just turned five. Big party."

"Enough to warrant fifty Mylar balloons? Musta been some celebration."

John Tapp's focus alternates from Lucy's face to Lew's. He spreads his arms wide. "Look, folks, don't worry. Guess we shoulda told you. Remember this show is UFOs: Hoax or Real? Well, you were chosen for the hoax segment." He gestures to his cameramen and steps away. Their red lights come on. Lucy and Lew are left standing alone in the spotlight.

All of a sudden a different kind of light flashes across the sky. It's bright and fast as a shooting star but too close and too big for that. More come. Zoom. Zoom. They cross the sky, coming from west to east, east to west, north to south… Lucy stares at the heavens, her mouth gaping. "Where'd Cousin Larry get those?"

John Tapp ducks. "Hey," he shouts, "are these things dangerous?"

A sound fills the sky, so deep and low that everything for miles vibrates. Lew feels the hairs on his arms rise. Above the jetting lights a larger light has appeared. Its brilliance sheds an iridescent Day-glo green across the landscape.

John Tapp looks at Lew. "What's going on here?"

Lew stares at the descending light, speechless. The temperature of the air has risen at least thirty degrees. He feels his face burning.

John Tapp takes one last look upward, then he and his camera crew run for their lives.

"You think it's Grandma?" Lucy whispers. She and Lew drop to their knees, their faces shining. At any moment they expect to see stairs descend. At any moment they expect to see Grandma return from outer space.

Unfortunately, that's not exactly what happens.

*　　　*　　　*

Ten years later the billboard off Interstate 70 reads, "Site of the 2012 Space Craft Landing." The UFO Motel has been replaced by the Laredo Spa and Resort, a luxurious country club run by who else but Cousin Larry. He's switched from the wife beater T-shirt and the dirty levis to silk Khakis and Tommy Bahama, flowered shirts. Hundreds flock to his resort where they can golf, swim, get a facial or a message, and for only fifty dollars journey by van out into the desert and witness the very place where the space craft landed. The heat from the famous UFO melted the sand where Lew and Lucy Laredo were standing, incasing the couple in glass, and if you look down at the spot, you will see the petrified remains of the two staring up at you, preserved forever like bugs in amber.

The Salty Sea Resort

Buzzards soar high above the Great Salt Sea buffeted by the hot winds off the desert. Beneath them speed boats pulling water skiers make broad figure eights. Trailer parks dot the shoreline and there's a brand, new resort, The Great Salt Yacht Club. Dozens of swimmers frolic in the water near its pier, buoyed up by the high saline content. Some claim it's so salty you could walk on it. Others notice the odor. Something dead, and that's why the buzzards are here.

Twenty years later and the same buzzards are flying over the same desert sea only things have changed. The site of the former Great Salt Yacht Club is now nothing more than fallen boards and cement slab. The pier has collapsed into the water. The sea itself has shrunk and there are more dead fish. Lots more.

Speeding west through the desert in their brand new pink 1970 Coupe de Ville, Rocky and Flo Montana notice the giant billboard just about the same time Rocky realizes they're almost out of gas. "Visit the Salty Sea Resort," says the billboard, and underneath that, "Once You're Here, You'll Never Leave." There's a picture of a speed boat pulling a water-skier—a blonde, her hair flowing in the wind. She's wearing a canary yellow, two-piece bathing suit, and a great big smile.

Rocky slaps the steering wheel. "Dang, should have gassed up this morning before we left." His eyes take a quick survey of the surrounding landscape—nothing but barren desert dotted with a few dried-up bushes and an occasional cactus.

Flo fans her face. "Did you see that billboard? There must be a lake out here somewhere." She pulls her damp blouse away from her chest. "Boy, I sure could use a swim."

Ahead is another smaller sign that says, "Great Salt Sea." An arrow points to the right. Rocky brakes and takes the turn-off.

Flo stubs out her cigarette. "Oh, goodie. I love an adventure."

"Let's just hope they got gas," Rocky mutters.

The narrow two-lane road snakes out into the desert. After about a mile, it becomes a one lane, the pavement broken and potholed. Not much further the surface turns to dirt.

Rocky squints through the clouds of dust. "Where'n hell is this place, anyway?" He's turned off the air conditioning to save gas, and it's hotter than Hades inside the car. Finally, they descend over a rise and see a line of blue in the distance. Rocky can make out a palm tree and some buildings and neon signs too faraway to read. Three miles more and they come to a gas station—two pumps shaded by a cement overhang. The station itself is tiny and dusty and one of its windowpanes is missing. Off to the right a group of identical white cottages sit all in a row. There's a larger one just like the rest with a big neon sign on top that reads, "Salty Sea Motel."

Rocky lowers his car window and surveys the dusty gas pump. "Dang. Looks like this place is dead."

Flo peers at her husband over the top of her rhinestone-studded sunglasses. "What're we gonna do?" The henna of her furrowed eyebrows exactly matches her dyed, red hair.

Rocky opens the car door, scoots his belly from behind the pink steering wheel, and gets out with a grunt. "I'm gonna go see if there's a phone booth around here." With a stiff gait he crosses to the tiny building and disappears around in back. He returns to the car a minute later, leans in the window, and informs his wife, "I found a phone booth, but the phone's dead." He squints toward the line of blue in the distance, lights a cigarette, then gets back into the car.

"Welcome to the Salty Sea Resort."

Rocky never even saw the man approach. All of a sudden he was just there, leaning down, looking into the driver's side window. A light breeze blows his fine blond hair, exposing his sunburned scalp. He has the same light hair on his arms, and they're sunburned, too. He smiles and that's when Rocky notices his eyes. One's normal, but the other looks like it might pop right out of his head. The man straightens and steps back. A whistle escapes his cracked lips as he takes in Rocky and Flo's car. "Well. Well. Never seen a pink Caddy afore."

Rocky gestures with his thumb. "Little woman here works for Mary Kay. You know, Mary Kay Cosmetics?" Rocky winks at Flo. "She was number one in sales three years straight."

"You don't say." The man's normal eye focuses on Rocky, but the bulging one is off somewhere else. Rocky averts his gaze.

The man looks over the car again. "My. My."

Rocky glances at Flo. "'Course the color wouldn't have been my first choice. Titty pink. You'd think—"

Flo sticks out her lower lip. "Ahhh, hon. I like the color."

"Don't get me wrong." Rocky beams at his wife. "I'm proud as punch of Flo."

The stranger smiles, but only with his good eye. The other one gives off a dull, flat glare. "Where you folks from?"

"Florida." Rocky looks straight ahead to avoid staring at the man's weird eye. "We're headed for L.A. Hollywood." He grins. "Little bride here wants to see some movie stars." He points at the rusty tanks. "Got any gas?"

"Sure thing," the man says.

"Fill it with supreme, would ya?"

"Okey dokey." While the gas tank's filling, the man takes a damp rag and goes to work on the dusty windshield. He checks under the hood, slams it shut, and returns. "Everything looks okay." He puts out his palm. "At'll be nine eighty five."

Rocky hands him a ten dollar bill. "Keep the change." He turns the key in the ignition. The engine coughs a couple of times and dies. He tries again. More coughing, and then nothing. The man hasn't moved.

"Was the radiator full?" Rocky asks him.

The fellow frowns. "Seemed okay. You want, I'll have another look." He lifts the lid and putters around under the hood for a minute. Rocky is about to get out and join him when the man returns. "Distributor's bad."

"What?" Rocky straight-arms the steering wheel. "But this is a brand, new car." He frowns. "You sure you didn't jiggle something when you were under there? Maybe a wire came loose?" Rocky's always wished he knew more about cars.

The man gives Rocky a straight-on look with his good eye. "Nuh uh. I know my caddys." He nods his head. "Yes sirree. That I do."

Rocky sighs. "Well, you think you can fix it?"

The man frowns. "Maybe. I'll have to call over to Furnace City. See if they have a distributor." He turns to go. "Be back in a shake."

Flo watches the man as he heads down the dusty road toward the Salty Sea Motel. "You think he'll be able to help us?"

Rocky tugs at his damp shirt which is clinging to his chest. "Sure hope so."

"Whatcha think of that strange eye?"

Rocky shrugs. "Don' know. Maybe he's got thyroid or something."

Fifteen minutes pass. Rocky and Flo emerge from the car into the burning heat. A blast of hot wind off the desert ruffles Flo's fiery red hair. It blows Rocky's comb-over exposing his Florida-tanned pate. His gaze wanders off toward the line of white cottages. "Wonder what's taking so long." He's about to set off in that direction, when he sees the gas station owner returning. From a distance the man's light hair blends right into the landscape. His outline shimmers like a mirage in the heat.

He approaches Rocky and Flo and extends his arm. "Mechanic over in Furnace City has a distributor, but he won't be able to get it here 'til tomorrow." He points in the direction of the Salty Sea Motel where a buzzard has landed on the neon sign. "Must be your lucky day." He gives them a cracked-lip smile, his gimpy eye staring into space. "Cottage five is available."

*   *   *

Rocky and Flo emerge from their cottage into the crackling heat. Rocky's wearing bright blue bathing trunks and a Hawaiian shirt covered with fiery orange hibiscus blossoms. He carries their two beach chairs plus a couple of the motel's skimpy white towels. Their cottage was a little on the skimpy side too—nothing but a wooden chair and table in need of varnish, and a queen-sized bed. He and Flo prefer king. Flo perked up, though, when she saw the photo on the wall—a beach scene. She swore the two leaning against the backrests in the sand were Marilyn Monroe and Clark Gable.

Rocky crosses the dirt road and stands, gazing up and down at the seven cottages. In front of the first is a 1950's woody Ford station wagon, all the varnish worn off. In front of the second is a Chevy Impala, its green paint giving way to the gray primer beneath. An old Ford pickup with rusted bumpers and four flat tires sits in front of the third. Rocky looks up and down. "Wonder where all the folks are."

Flo stands on the threshold and follows Rocky's gaze. Her lacy cover-up is open in front, exposing her new lavender bikini and her not-so-new rolls of flab. Rocky lied when he told her she looked good in the bathing suit, but what the hell. Isn't that what a husband's supposed to do? Flo shades her eyes and gazes toward the patch of blue in the distance. "Maybe they've all gone to the beach."

Rocky and Flo set off in that direction.

After what he estimates has been at least a half a mile of walking, Rocky stops in the middle of the dirt road and lowers the beach chairs to the ground. Around them is nothing but desert sand and sagebrush. He removes his sunglasses and wipes his brow. "Damn, it's hot. We shoulda stayed put in the motel room."

Flo gazes in the direction of the Great Salt Sea. "But hon, you know I love the beach."

Above them the dried brown fronds of a palm tree rustle in the hot breeze. A little further along, and they begin to notice the smell, kind of fishy mixed with something rangy-like and dead. Rocky stops. "Geez, Flo. You sure you wanta go here?"

She keeps walking. As they get closer, clumps of gray-green brush rise up nearly blocking their view of the water. A few more steps and the road ends right at the beach. Up close the Salty Sea has lost its nice blue color. The smell of its brackish brown waters makes Rocky want to gag.

Flo shades her eyes and gazes up and down the beach. "Oh, myyyy." A little ways away an abandoned sofa sits facing the water. Springs are poking out of its cushions, and the stuffing's coming out. Further down the beach are the remains of an abandoned building, a few boards sticking up out of the sand.

They walk in that direction and come upon a pile of bones, bleached white by the sun. They're stacked one upon the other, radiating out from the center like some kind of weird shrine.

"What the heck?" Rocky points to a wooden box lying in the sand a few feet away. At first he thinks it's a coffin, but on closer inspection, he realizes it's a grandfather clock. It's lying flat on its back, one of its brass balls dangling over the edge onto the sand. The glass in the door covering the dials is broken. Rocky blinks. Did that minute hand just move?

Flo frowns. "I wonder who'd leave a thing like this on a beach."

Rocky's wondering the same thing.

"Well I don't care." She kicks off her sandals and minces toward the water. Rocky drops the beach chairs and stays put.

Flo points at a pile of something dark at the water's edge. She holds her nose and looks back at her husband. "Dead fish."

She approaches the water and dips in her big toe. "Ugh." Her voice lowers. "It's boiling hot." She returns and stands by her husband. The two gaze up and down the beach.

"I wonder where all the people are." Flo sounds wistful.

"Are you kidding?" Rocky barks. "Who'd wanta come to this hell-hole?"

"But what about that billboard? And those cars in front of the cabins back at the motel?" She fakes like she's about to cry. "I thought this place was gonna be fun."

Rocky eyes the grandfather clock and shrugs. "Beats me."

Buzzards circle above them, riding the thermals high into the sky.

*   *   *

Rocky climbs the one step to the motel office. With the setting sun behind him, he can't see through the screen door, but he can hear the hum of the fan. The screen squeaks open a little and the white-haired man with the gimpy eye stands facing him. Whitey's the man's name. Rocky learned that when he signed the register earlier.

"Uh, ya have any vending machines?" Rocky asks. "Me and the wife, we're a little hungry, and being as we don't have a car—"

Whitey opens the screen door wider and motions for Rocky to come in. He leads Rocky from the front office, which is essentially bare, through a door into what seems to be a small warehouse. Every square inch of space is so jam-packed with stuff that there's barely room to stand. A tower of assorted Styrofoam and metal coolers rises above a clutter of suitcases in various shapes and sizes, stacks of clothes, dresses, men's pants, a bright orange Hawaiian shirt, a pair of pink sandals… Rocky spots the bottoms of a canary yellow two-piece bathing suit that reminds him of the two-piece on the babe on the billboard. Nearby are some five gallon cans of paint. The lid of one is encrusted in dried canary yellow. There's food, too, boxes of cornflakes, Bisquick, a large jar of Del Monte pickles…

Whitey makes a broad gesture with his arm. "It's all for sale. Just name your price."

Rocky examines a framed collage under glass that hangs from the wall. They're some bleached white rocks inside and a lot of small bones. Painted on the wood backing of the collage is a beach scene and glued on top of that is a magazine photo of a grandfather clock. Rocky studies it, scratching his head. No accounting for some people's taste.

"You like it?" Whitey asks.

Rocky strokes his chin. "Well."

"It's not for sale."

Rocky's eyes roam the room. He notices a figure in a wicker chair in the corner—an older woman with very pink skin and perfectly white hair. He barely saw her behind the stack of cardboard boxes. She's sitting so still that at first he mistook her for a mannequin. She gives him a vacant stare.

Whitey bats the air. "Oh, don't worry about her. That's just Mother."

Rocky nods. "How do, ma'am."

She moves her lips, but no sound comes out.

"Fried her vocal chords," Whitey informs Rocky. "Draino."

*   *   *

Flo, in nothing but her bra and panties, is lying on the bed reading Cosmopolitan when Rocky returns. She's done her flaming red hair up in spongy pink rollers. Above her the ceiling fan whirrs round and round.

Rocky throws a giant-sized bag of Laura Scudders potato chips onto the bed. "This was about all I could find," he tells her. "And these cans of Coke." He removes them from under his arm. "'Fraid they're not cold." He smiles. "We add enough of my Wild Turkey, though." He winks at Flo. "You'll never know what hit you."

She frowns at the bag of chips. "Guess it's better'n nothing."

Rocky begins fiddling with the T.V. and the rabbit ears, but he can't get anything but snow. "Weird deal over there at the office," he tells his wife. "Got some kinda warehouse going. You never seen so much stuff." He scratches his head. "That Whitey fellow's kinda odd. Met his mother. She can't talk. Won't believe what this guy told me…"

*   *   *

Rocky, soaking with sweat, wakes and sees the silhouette of his wife standing in the starlit doorway. He sits up. "What's going on?"

She takes a drag off her cigarette. "I can't sleep. It's too hot." She's still in just her bra and panties, her belly rolling over the top.

"Someone might see you standin' there, sugar. Don't you think you should come away from the door?"

She exhales a long, steady stream of smoke. "Aw, who'n hell's gonna see me here? This place is a ghost town." She's slurring her words. Probably the Wild Turkey.

Rocky thinks about Whitey possibly lurking about but decides to say nothing. The fan's stopped moving. He stands on the mattress and fiddles with the pull chain. "Must be busted," he mutters.

Flo comes back inside and sits down on the bed. "I can't sleep in this heat." She rises. "I'm going for a walk."

Rocky glances at his wrist. "At one in the morning?" He sits on the bed watching as she changes into her bikini and throws on her sandals. "Honey, I don't think this is such a—"

"—I don' care. I'm going." She staggers out of the room and down the steps.

Rocky shakes his head. Woman's always had a mind of her own. Cursing his stiff joints, he changes into his swimming trunks and a T-shirt. Outside it's still at least ninety degrees. The starlight's so bright, the palm tree is casting a shadow. In the distance he catches sight of Flo's bikini-clad figure weaving down the road toward the beach. Rocky hobbles after her. By the time he reaches the end of the road, he's soaked with sweat. It feels like the humidity's risen, and it magnifies the stench. A ways down the beach in a different direction from where they went earlier, Rocky sees Flo. She's standing stock still staring. As Rocky gets nearer, he sees what she's looking at. There at the water's edge stands a woman with hair so white it actually glows in the dark. Rocky squints. Whitey's mother? What could she possibly be doing down here at this time of night?

Rocky catches up with Flo who still hasn't moved. She points. "Is that a ghost?" Her words aren't slurring anymore.

The woman with the white hair hugs herself and sways in the moonlight.

"I think it's Whitey's mother," Rocky whispers. "Maybe she's lost."

The woman raises her head and beckons to them. They stare back. She beckons again.

"Guess we oughta go see what she wants," Rocky says.

When they reach the old woman, she points at a place in the sand. It's another one of the bone monuments like they saw earlier when they came to the beach. She motions for Rocky and Flo to follow and stops at another pile of bones, only this time the bones are bigger.

"What's the deal with the bones?" Flo asks.

Rocky shakes his head. "Dunno."

A little further down the beach and more bones. They're everywhere. Sitting off to the right by itself in the sand is a skull. Rocky wonders if it's human. His pulse quickens. Something's not right around here. The old woman points at a shack that stands up from the beach near a clump of bushes. She motions. As they near the tiny structure, Rocky notices something white gleaming in the open doorway. Bones. Crickets chirp in the bushes. The sound is growing louder and louder. The rhythm is like a ticking clock. Rocky puts a hand on Flo's arm and stops. "I don't know, Flo. There's something kinda funny goin' on."

Whitey's mother stands beside the open door and motions frantically. Rocky shrugs and moves forward. When he and

Flo are within a few steps of the shack, Whitey's mother steps just inside. The whir of the crickets has grown deafening and so high-pitched you want to plug your ears. Rocky senses something and spins around.

There standing right behind him is Whitey, his hair florescent in the moonlight. He's wearing that weird smile of his where one eye crinkles and the other one stares into space. In his hand a silver blade gleams. He raises his arm. "Welcome to the Salty Sea Resort."

* * *

Buzzards soar high above the Salty Sea Motel buffeted by the hot winds off the desert. Seven cottages stand all in a row. In front of number one is a 1950 Ford Station wagon, its wood weathered and rough. Next door at number two is a Chevy Impala. Its paint is peeling off. In front of number five sits a 1970 Coupe De Ville. It used to be pink, but over the years the color's slowly faded to white.

Speeding west through the desert in their brand new 1982 Ford Mustang, Fred and Carrie Goldsmith see the billboard just about the same time Fred realizes they're almost out of gas.

Welcome to the Salty Sea Resort.

Prey

An owl raced its shadow across Larsen's Valley. In the moonlit meadow far below, a chipmunk poked its head out of its hole. The little animal never felt a thing, not even the air move. With a flap of its great wings the owl soared back up into the sky, its prey dangling from its claws.

The owl banked left, passing over the exact same field where Sydney Sue St. John's naked body lay perfect and pure and white in the moonlight. The owl flew straight, following the line of Rural Route 36. Beneath it a 1955 Nash Rambler carrying fourteen-year-old Francie Fulton and her sixteen-year-old companion Lola Nelson sped along. Two girls out on a Friday night. Just looking for fun.

Rock music blasted from the open car windows, echoing through the trees and out into the night. "Oh, my friends call me Speedo, but my real name is…" Francie tapped her fingers on the dashboard as she sang along, her heart racing to keep up with the music. She'd talked her neighbor Lola into driving, and they'd taken Francie's mother's car, and if they got caught, Francie was going to be in the most trouble she'd ever been in in her entire life.

Trees zipped past in the moonlight. Every so often a billboard advertising Pall Malls or Pabst Blue Ribbon flew by. Francie cringed as she counted the sins she was committing. Taking her mother's car was the worst. Then there was the lying and going to the drive-in which was not permitted because Francie was only fourteen. Add to that hanging out with Lola. Everyone in town said Lola was *fast*. And then there were the sins Francie was planning to commit, like smoking cigarettes, flirting with boys, maybe even kissing one, older boys too, not those juveniles that went to her school. She was so excited she could just die.

The glow in the distance grew brighter.

Friday night and Oscars was hopping. Cars radiated in concentric circles around the brightly lit building. On its roof sat a giant cow, its tongue licking the milkshake mustache from its upper lip. It wore a red gingham apron and held up a tall glass between its cloven hooves. Lola circled the outer perimeter of the parking lot twice before making an abrupt left at the end of a row of cars. Francie gasped as the passenger side of her mother's Nash Rambler barely missed the right fender of a metallic blue Ford. The way Lola had kept slipping over the white line back there on the highway made Francie wonder if she really did have her driver's license after all. Too late now, and anyway they were here, and this was going to be the most wonderful night of Francie's entire life.

Lola pulled in behind a white Chevy convertible, came to an abrupt stop, and turned off the ignition. She leaned forward and scanned the cars then leaned back and folded her arms. Francie turned her head from side to side, then flopped back against the seat and folded her arms too. A boy in the car on Lola's side leaned his head out the window. "Lola. Loow La." He made his voice deep and low, like a cow bawling for its babies.

Lola scooted over to the center of the front seat to where she could look at her face in the rearview mirror. She ran her baby finger over the pouty points of her passion pink upper lip, then licked her fingers and adjusted a curl.

"Loow La," the blonde guy moaned.

She completely ignored him.

Francie, keeping her eyes pointed straight forward, tried to make her voice sound casual. "So, do you know him?"

Lola rolled her dark brown eyes. "Barely." The grayish smudges beneath them gave her a sleepy, sultry look. Francie wondered if with makeup she could achieve the same thing. Lola began turning the dial on the radio, screeching past stations faster than a hotrod being chased by the police. She stopped when she got it on the same station that the surrounding cars were playing.

A waitress wearing a red hat and a short gingham skirt leaned in the window. She cracked her gum. "Ya wanna order?"

Lola shook her head. "Nah, maybe later." With that she leaped out of the car, climbed onto the hood, and struck a pose, her body swaying to the music coming from the other cars. She wore yellow polka-dot capris and an ivory cashmere sweater that fit over her pointy breasts snug as two socks. Francie glanced down at her own plain white blouse with the Peter Pan collar. She hated the kind of clothes her mother made her wear. She hated the stupid rules. She hated all the *Jesus loves you* stuff. No wonder her older sister Nora ran off. Francie was just eleven when it happened, and Nora was seventeen. There was this pachuco named Carlos. Their mother told Nora she couldn't see him, so Nora just up and left.

Francie adjusted the bow on her ponytail. She'd wanted to get her hair cut in a ducktail. It was the latest style, but her mother said girls shouldn't wear their hair that short. People might think you were a boy. God, she was so square. Francie could just picture her sitting at their kitchen table, the top edges of her pale pink cardigan held together by that stupid plastic gold chain, her baby sweet voice. "Now, Francine…" Sometimes she made Francie want to die.

Francie's dad wasn't so bad, but he wasn't so good either. He just wasn't anything. He came home from work every day, got his beer and his newspaper and barely said boo. "That's nice," he'd said once when Francie showed him the A she'd gotten on her short story. Mr. Buckworth, the English teacher, told Francie she had talent. She hated Mr. Buckworth's bad breath and the hairs that stuck out of his nose, but she loved talking to him about books.

Francie watched Lola on the hood of her mother's car. A group of friends had gathered, mostly girls, all kids Lola's age. Francie doubted any of her friends would be here. Oscars was pretty much taboo for junior high kids. Francie'd come here once, though. It was during the day, and one of her friend's mothers drove. There were a lot of truckers. Francie hated the way they looked at her—the winks, the leers. You could tell they had something dirty on their minds.

Francie tucked the corners of her blouse back into her skirt, opened the car door, and slowly got out. She wasn't sure if it was okay for her to join Lola. These were older kids. They might not want her around. Most of them were smoking. Maybe if Francie lit up, she'd fit in too.

"Uh," she tapped the elbow of a curly-haired redhead. "Think I could bum a ciggy?" The redhead looked down at Francie and scowled. "Huh?"

Francie gestured. "I'm with Lola."

"Ohhhh," the redhead replied. "Well, in that case." She offered Francie one of her L & M's, lit it for her, then turned away.

Francie tapped her on the shoulder. "Say, I really like your skirt."

The redhead glanced down at her blue felt poodle skirt and smiled showing her dimples. "You do?"

"I sure do." Francie breathed.

The redhead patted the fender beside her. "Come on. Have a seat."

Francie took quick, short drags off her cigarette, careful not to inhale too deeply. The first time she'd tried smoking she'd drawn in a huge lungful and coughed for ten minutes. Not for anything was she going to look like an amateur now. Cupping her elbow in her left hand, she took another puff, curled her tongue, and slowly let it out. She'd inhaled a little. It made her feel jumpy inside, like something really exciting was about to happen.

The boy standing next to Lola winked at Francie. Lola noticed and glared.

A short, plump girl wearing lots of petticoats came racing up, breathless. "You guys hear about Sydney Sue St. John?" She surveyed the sea of eager faces. "She's missing. The police have been all over our street."

The girl behind Lola piped up. "Sydney Sue's in my Science class. She told me she hates her mother. Maybe she ran away."

Like Nora? Francie wondered what ever became of her sister. They hadn't heard a word in two years.

The curly-haired redhead nudged Francie. She nodded at the car parked just behind them on their right. "You know that guy?"

Francie followed the girl's gaze to a black sedan that had been lowered in front. Sure enough, the guy in the driver's seat was staring straight at her. Francie took just a quick glance, barely long enough to see that he had coal black hair greased back on the sides and a sausage curl that fell down over his forehead. His long narrow face was shaped like a *v*. He looked too old to go to her school. There was another guy in the front seat too, but Francie couldn't see him at all.

"Do they go to Washington High?" Francie asked the redhead.

The girl frowned. "I don't know." She took a quick glance that way. "I don't think so." She nudged Francie again and giggled. Francie glanced over. The guy was still staring.

"How old do you think he is?" Francie asked.

Casually the redhead turned and looked. "Seventeen, maybe even eighteen." She shook her head. "I can't tell."

Wow, eighteen. Francie couldn't avoid another glance. The guy blew her a kiss that lasted so long Francie squirmed and had to turn away.

A few kids ordered Cokes and one of the boys passed around a little bottle in a brown paper bag. "Seagrams," the redhead whispered. She offered Francie a sip. Francie'd never tasted liquor before. She wasn't sure she liked it, but it was exciting and different, and she couldn't wait to tell her friends at school. Every so often she would take a quick peek back at the other car, and every time the guy with the greasy black hair would be staring. They'd lock eyes, and Francie's heart would leap. It was hard to look away. All of a sudden, he turned on his car and revved the engine. It made a booming sound that could have been heard for miles around. Still gunning the engine, he moved the car to the right. It quivered like a horse being reined in when it wants to run. Slowly the black car pulled forward. With one last glance at Francie from the driver, they took off.

Francie didn't know whether to be sad or glad that he was gone. She'd never had a boy look at her like that before. It made her feel kind of jittery inside, and scared and good and bad all at the same time. Gradually some of the kids began to drift away.

Lola was still with the same guy, the one who'd winked at Francie. The two started to walk off.

"I gotta be home by ten," Francie called after them.

Lola nodded so Francie assumed she'd heard.

Pretty soon even the redheaded girl said she had to leave. Francie got back into the car and sat waiting. A waitress walked down the aisle. "Last orders," she called out. Francie glanced at her watch. Oh, my God, she had no idea it was eleven thirty already. Where was Lola? Why hadn't she come back?

The waitresses were all piling into cars and leaving. One by one the lights inside Oscars went off.

Where was Lola?

In the distance an owl hooted. Francie shivered and rolled up her window just a bit. Gone was the sound of rock music. The aroma of French fries no longer lingered in the air. A cool breeze drifted in through the car window bringing with it the scent of skunk and pine needles and the night. The only car left in the parking lot was another Nash Rambler. Through its rear window Francie could see a boy and a girl making out. At quarter after midnight they left too. Francie didn't know what to do. She couldn't walk home. It was too far, and even if Francie had considered trying to drive her mother's car, she couldn't have because Lola had taken the keys. Why, why had she ever trusted Lola? This was all a stupid idea. She never should have come.

Francie was just fishing around in her purse for some change to call her mother when she heard the car's engine.

Heart beating, she glanced behind her. It was the black sedan, the one with the driver who'd been staring at her all evening. He pulled up right beside her with his window rolled down, so close she could practically feel his breath, so close their cars we're almost touching.

"Well, well, lookie who's here," he said. There were tiny lines between his eyebrows. Close up he looked way older than he had before. "Your friend run off and leave you?" he asked.

Francie shrugged. "Uh, I guess so. Sorta." She could see the other guy in the car now. He looked way older and kind of creepy, and she didn't like the grin on his face. Her eyes scanned the dark parking lot. She'd have felt a lot better if there were other people around.

"I'm Lennie Love." The driver with the black hair made a little sideways jerk of his chin at the passenger beside him. "And this here's Floyd Hardy." Lennie Love offered his hand out the window for Francie to shake.

She just looked at it.

He retrieved his hand, palm up, and smiled. He returned his focus to Francie, his dark eyes probing. "So here's the plan, doll. How 'bout Floyd and me we drive you home?"

Francie tried to look away, but she couldn't. "Uh, I don't think so," she whispered. Was she being stupid? Maybe she *should* let them give her a ride home.

"Ah, honey. Pretty little thing like you. Now don't be afraid."

She looked down at her trembling hands. What should she do?

"C'mon Francie Fulton. You and me we're gonna be good friends."

Francie gulped. "How'd you know my name?"

He raised his palms. "Ah, honey. I'm Lennie Love." He said it real long and low. "I know it allllll."

"Uh, I think maybe you'd better leave." Francie rolled up her window.

The black car leaped forward, jerked to a stop, and Lennie Love jumped out. Quick, Francie locked her car door, then slid over and rolled up the window on the driver's side. Barely in time she locked that door too. Lennie Love leaped onto the hood of her car. From inside Francie felt it shudder. He crouched on all fours and peered down at her through the moonlit windshield, the glow in his black eyes forcing her to return his gaze. "Now, here's what I want you to do, Francie." He stuck his finger in his mouth then slowly pulled it out. He held it up as if to test the breeze. "I-want-you-to—" He said each word slowly. "—unlock the door and get out of the car." He gestured toward his companion who stood a few feet away. "See Floyd, here? He wants to be your friend, too." Floyd was taller than any man Francie ever knew. He had a little roll of flab around his stomach and the whitest skin she'd ever seen.

"Please, go," Francie whimpered.

Lennie turned down the corners of his mouth. "Ah, Francie, sweetheart, now don't say that. Everything's gonna be all right. You'll see." He got down off the car and came around to stand by her window, crouching low so he could look straight into her eyes.

"C'mon, Francie, open up the door."

She shook her head. If only she could take her eyes away from his.

A slow, smooth smile glided across his face. "I can tell you're the kind of girl who's gonna like it." He nodded. "Girls like you always do." He raised his palms and looked at the sky. "I'm Lennie Love, and I know all about that goodness that's hidden deep inside you." He winked. "And I'm gonna find it, and you're gonna like it a lot when I do."

Standing a little ways away in the moonlight, Floyd ran the flat of his palm gently across his crotch.

"C'mon, Francie," Lennie beckoned with his finger.

She covered her ears and shook her head. "Stop it. Please, please, stop it." She pictured her mother at this moment, sitting there at the kitchen table, her pale pink sweater held together by that gold chain. "Now, where could Francine possibly be?" Francie thought about her own bedroom upstairs, the pastel curtains with the little lambs embroidered all over them, the picture of Jesus hanging on the wall. If Francie ever got back there, she'd never go away again. Not ever.

She opened her eyes, and there was Lennie Love still staring. He cocked his head. A sad, sweet smile spread across his face. "C'mon now, Francie. I know you can do it. Open up the door."

She shook her head.

His voice wouldn't stop. "I know all about that sweet, secret place deep inside you. I know you better than you know your own self. Come on now, honey, open up. Let Lennie Love into your heart."

As if it weren't her own, Francie's hand crept toward the door handle.

Lennie watched it, whispering, "C'mon. C'mon."

Her fingers touched the handle, felt the cold line of steel.

"That's it," Lennie whispered, "You're gonna like it when you get on out here. I promise. You're gonna be begging Lennie Love for more and more."

Francie's mother's voice filled her head as she got out of the car. *Jesus loves you.*

Loner

Standing on the banks of the Madison River along about Ennis, you can follow the river's upstream flow miles and miles eastward through gold and lime-green meadows to where it disappears into the lavender folds of the far-off mountains. In the fields away from the river, a few horses dot the hillside. There's a barbed-wire fence to keep them in, and a barn, and a sprawling farmhouse, but not many man-made structures other than that. Well, there are a few shacks around like that one that sits on the slope up there, just down the embankment from the highway. Its metal roof sags on one side. The planks of its front steps are weathered practically through. Strangers to the area assume it's abandoned, for who on earth would choose to live in the middle of nowhere in such a rundown hovel as that? Who except for maybe a *woodtick*. That's the label folks in Montana give to loners who abide in the woods all by themselves.

The sun is halfway toward setting over the Tobacco Root Mountains. The only sound to jar the stillness is the moan of an eighteen-wheeler up on the highway, shifting gears as it climbs the hill. A male figure steps out onto the porch of the rundown shack. Clad in dusty levis and a bleach-splotched snap shirt, his scrawny frame is perfectly camouflaged against the shaded background of his abode. He stands five feet nine inches tall, slightly splay-footed in his sharp-toed cowboy boots. Mathew Valentine's his name. He tends horses down on the ranch. A solitary line of work. He likes it that way.

The boards beneath his feet creak like old saddle leather as he descends the steps. Chickens pecking the ground near the bottom of the stairs move aside to let him pass. A gust of air stirs the skivvies on his clothesline and causes his shirt to swing back and forth. With a slow and slightly bow-legged gait he starts down a well-worn path that descends from the mountainside to the meadow below. The sound of neighing drifts up to meet him. Dinnertime, and the horses are hungry. They know he's coming. He always does.

The moon has risen. The stars are beginning to come out when Mathew trudges back up the mountain. As he approaches the cabin he catches sight of lights up on the highway. Closer, and he catches the faint sound of voices drifting down. Strange for someone to be walking along the road at this time of night or even in the daytime for that matter. Not many people around these parts except for the family who owns the ranch.

They come in the summer, bring their kids, and do a lot of fishing and horseback riding. Mathew saddles their horses in the morning before they've even eaten their pancakes. Then by the time they come down to the stables, he's long gone.

The voices up on the highway are getting closer. Is that the silhouette of a man or a woman up there on the ridge? Quickly Mathew climbs the stairs onto his porch and lets himself into the dark cabin. If he doesn't turn on a light, hopefully whoever it is up there on the road won't even take notice. He doesn't mind helping out if there's an emergency, but sometimes people come bothering him with car problems that they really could take care of themselves.

He's brewing a pot of coffee by candlelight when he hears a voice. "Hello, anyone home?"

Inwardly he groans. No choice now but to open the door and see who's there.

At the bottom of the stairs, a woman and two kids gaze up at him, their faces pale in the starlight. The smaller one's a boy and he's hanging onto what must be his older sister's hand. "Sorry to disturb you—" The woman's voice is meek. "—but we've had a flat tire up there on the highway and—" She raises her hand, gripping a cell phone. "—I can't get reception."

That's exactly what Mathew's sister Nancy is always complaining about. Calls this place the boonies. Claims it's not safe.

Mathew studies the three, shifting from foot to foot. He could offer to change their tire, but—

"Do you think I could use your land line to call the Auto Club?" the woman asks.

He lets out sigh of relief. She's right. Better to let the Auto Club take care of it. He opens the screen door and beckons to the three to come on up.

The girl—Mathew'd put her in her early teens—turns to what must be her mother and says something low that he can't hear. "It's okay," her mother tells her. Mathew senses their fear. He winces slightly and averts his gaze. He's waiting to hear the whispered word. Woodtick. Thankfully it doesn't come.

A loose board creaks as they climb the steps up to the porch. The little boy has gizmos on the heels of his shoes that light up when he walks—type of thing a kid that age would love. Mathew's tempted to comment, but can't decide exactly what he'd say. Instead he flips on the switch just inside the door.

A circle of light beams down from the ceiling, leaving the corners of the cabin mostly in darkness. The three newcomers glance around the room—at the heap of dirty clothes near the sofa, at the shotgun leaning against the wall nearby, at the stacks and stacks of canned goods reaching almost to the ceiling. Mathew stocks up at the Vons over in Boseman every three months. Means he eats a lot of Chef Boyardee and

Dinty Moore, but he doesn't mind. Better than buying fresh stuff that would spoil, and then he'd only be able to buy a few weeks' supply at a time which would mean he'd have to go back more often, and there's nothing he hates worse than those chatty clerks in Vons.

He points at the phone on the wall next to the kitchen. The woman uses it to call the Auto Club. She talks to them a minute then hangs up. "They're not sure how soon someone can get out here. They said they'd call back in a few minutes." A frown creases her brow. "I hope it's okay that I told them they could call back on this number."

Mathew sighs and nods. A few minutes could mean a few hours. What then?

The woman goes over and stands beside the kids near the door.

The daughter glances at Mathew then asks her mother, "Can't we go wait outside?"

The mother puts a hand on the girl's shoulder, the other on the shoulder of the boy. "It's okay."

The three stare at Mathew, not saying a word. He figures he should offer them a seat, but all he's got is that beat-up leather sofa that used to be down in the ranch house. It smells like cat pee, and if he invites them to sit down, it will probably start a conversation, and then they might end up staying longer than is really necessary. The coffee pot percolates on the stove casting the rich scent of Yuban into the air. He glances in that direction, then back at the threesome, then down at the floor. If his sister Nancy were here, she'd be offering the woman coffee and the kids, glasses of milk. Before you know it they'd be deep in conversation. His sister loves to talk. It's not that Mathew doesn't like to talk. It's just that he doesn't see the point.

The little boy, must be about four or five, keeps glancing at the coffee table. Amid a copy of *The Call Of The Wild* which Mathew's read at least ten times, a set of clippers that he uses to trim his hair, and some fence nails stands a wire sculpture. It's a cowboy riding a bucking bronco. His sister Nancy makes them out of wire. She's managed to earn a living off her art. Just barely. Sells her stuff at gift stores throughout the western states. Her husband left her when Stevie, Mathew's nephew, was only three. Since then she's been all on her own. Not easy being a single mother.

"You can touch it if you want to." The words jump from Mathew's mouth before he even realizes what he's done. The three start at the sound of his voice. He feels the dreaded warmth spread up his neck.

The boy looks at his mother and points at the statue. "Can I?" he whispers. He's got curly blonde hair that hangs down his neck, a little girlish, but, heck, he's just a kid.

His mother smiles and nods. She's a bit stocky and her jeans fit her awful tight, but there's something kind of pretty about her long blonde hair, and there's a softness in her face that reminds Mathew of someone he used to know. He wonders if she's a single mom. The daughter is skinny and dark-haired and doesn't look at all like her mother. Cute though. If Mathew were her dad, he wouldn't let the boys anywhere near her.

The kid takes the two steps over to the coffee table, reaches out, and barely touches the sculpture. Nothing happens.

Mathew moves over beside him and drops down to his level. The crazy shoes he's got on have spider webs with eerie looking eyes on the sides. Mathew gives the rump of the bronco a little tap with his finger. The horse begins rocking back and forth as if it were bucking. The cowboy rocks back and forth, too. It's all a balancing thing.

The kid looks at Mathew and grins. Mathew can't help but smile back.

About then the phone rings. The Auto Club says they'll have someone there within the hour. From past experience Mathew knows that could mean three.

He draws a deep breath as he watches the trio start back up the dirt road to the highway. They said they'd go up and wait in their car. Mathew was tempted to suggest that they wait here, but then... Far off in the distance a lone wolf howls at the moon. Slowly Mathew turns and goes back inside his cabin.

*   *   *

Mathew glances at his alarm clock. 11:30 pm. Something woke him up. In the distance a pack of coyotes yip hysterically. He yawns, turns over and goes back to sleep. At 5 am he awakes again, this time to the sound of voices. It's got to be coming from up on the highway. A red ball bounces on and off his bedroom wall. Could it have taken this long for the Auto Club truck to get here? At five thirty he decides to get up and check things out.

The sun is just about to rise over the Gold Ridge Mountains as Mathew descends his porch steps. Done below the Madison River is still blanketed in mist. Up on the ridge a tow truck's red light is flashing. A pickup with its front mashed in is cabled to the tow truck's back end. Mathew climbs the dirt road to the highway to have a look.

A flatbed truck comes into view. On it are the crushed remains of a small compact car. What was once a Toyota Corolla is now nothing more than an accordion-pleated piece of metal no wider than a car door. Mathew stops and closes his eyes. Whoever was in that vehicle has to have been killed on impact. That must have been what wakened him at 11:30 last night, not the coyotes. He sure hopes that nice little family with the flat tire got out of here before all this happened.

Up on the pavement a highway patrolman and a couple of other guys are using brooms to sweep debris into a pile. Mathew recognizes one of the fellows, Roy the mechanic from the gas station down at Ennis. He looks up at Mathew with dead eyes. Mathew move closer and stops. There on the ground, scattered in amongst the shattered glass and pieces of broken metal are a plastic bottle of orange drink, the torn cover of People Magazine, a pair of pink cotton panties covered with red and purple hearts—God, he shouldn't be looking at this, but he can't stop—a woman's red slacks, a lavender comb coated with glitter, a paperback copy of *The Twilight Saga*, a toy plastic figure of Spiderman… He stares and stares. He can't take his eyes away. Jesus, the remains of some little family's lives. One second they're here. Next thing you know they're blasted into eternity. He imagines his nephew Stevie when Stevie was at the age to be playing with plastic figures. Cutest little kid you ever did see. Mathew always wished for a boy himself. Never even came close. Well, there was Cindy. She worked at the Broken Arrow Café down in Ennis. Mathew thought they had something going there for a while, but then she started complaining that he was too quiet, said he needed to liven up. It just didn't work out.

His eyes hit something unexpected. Stuck in a bush just a few inches from the pile of debris is a small shoe, black, with spider web markings on the side and an orange eye. "Oh, no." He covers his face and shakes his head. He never should have let them go back to their car. He should have made them wait right there in the cabin with him where it was safe.

Slowly he straightens. The wad in his throat is about to strangle him. He turns and gazes out over the valley, fighting the mist that threatens to blind his eyes.

Slowly he turns back to Roy.

"They were barely able to identify the bodies," Roy tells him. "A woman, maybe in her mid thirties, a teen girl, a boy around four or five. Didn't have a—"

"I know," Mathew says.

A big fellow wearing a reflector vest pulls out a trash bag and, using an industrial-sized dustbin, begins filling it with the debris.

Mathew raises his arm. "Stop!"

Roy and the man gape at him.

Mathew shrugs, blushing. He gestures at the pile in the road. "They might have family." His voice squeaks. "Someone might want this stuff."

The guy in the reflector vest grumbles a little, but finally agrees to let Mathew have one of his trash bags. Carefully, one by one, Mathew extracts the personal objects from the pile of debris.

*   *   *

Mathew sits on the leather couch in his cabin and stares at the trash bag on the floor. It's open just enough that he can see Spiderman's head and the purple hearts on the edge of the girl's pink panties. His sister Nancy called a little while ago. What timing. Mathew didn't tell her about the accident. She'd offer advice. Probably insist that he find the relatives and deliver to them the contents of the bag. Mathew rubs his forehead. Actually he'd thought of doing just that, but then, Oh God—bunch of strangers, probably talk his arm off and expect him to respond in kind. There'd be tears. What would he say?

"Nope." He stands and heads for the door. "Just can't do it."

Heading down to the stables, he's still thinking about the accident. Currying the horses, filling their water troughs, mucking out their stalls, it won't leave his mind. He lies in bed that night and see images of the two cars colliding, the pickup rounding the bend—maybe it swings a little too wide and pow. It slams into the Toyota. Did the kids feel anything? Did they know what was about to happen?

In the morning Mathew telephones Roy and asks if he knows anything about the girl's family. Are there relatives? Friends? Where's she from? Roy says he'll do a Google search and call Mathew back if he finds anything.

*   *   *

Turns out the gal's name was Allie Thompson. She was a waitress at the Truck Stop Café in Glendore a tiny town in the eastern part of the state. Mathew figures she may have been on a weekend visit to the Ennis area. Maybe meeting a boyfriend, something like that. She was a single mother, just as he'd expected. A waitress supporting two kids. It must have been rough. The daughter, her name Sharon, was just thirteen, the kid, Joey, only five.

Roy brought Mathew a printout of their obituaries. The daughter Sharon had just completed sixth grade, enjoyed the outdoors, playing softball, babysitting. You could tell she was a really good kid. And as for Joey—it said he loved riding his bicycle, and playing with his Thomas The Train set.

Mathew shifts his focus from the obituaries to the sack on the floor. It would be about a three hour drive to Glendore. He could do it and back in the same day. He'd never go if it meant an overnight. Then he'd have to stay in a motel, all those strangers to deal with, and, anyway, the horses couldn't stand to have him gone that long. He'd need to make sure the battery in the pickup's still charged. It hasn't been driven in about two months. Morning comes, and the gray mare's off her feed. Mathew decides to put off going to Glendore until the next day. The next day comes and he notices that Silver Star has developed a limp. A week passes. After spending a night tossing and turning and dreaming about the accident, he awakes one morning knowing it's time to go.

Splashes of gold and orange color the hillsides. The streams under a deep blue sky look almost black. About an hour and forty five minutes into the drive, Mathew realizes he's not even halfway. The horses. There's no choice but to turn around and go back. He pulls off the road just ahead of a bend in the grade that ascends the mountain and gets out. As he steps over to the rim of the valley to look at the view, something at the base of some scrub brush catches his eye—a wreath of yellow daisies, pink carnations and a white cross. Someone's placed them at the side of the road to memorialize a car accident. He never did anything for the three who died on the highway above his house. He gets back in the car and stares at the trash bag sagging over the edge of the passenger seat. If he hurries he can probably make it to Glendore and get back home by midnight. The horses should be okay.

The tiny town of Glendore sits on the intersection of 94 and 335. There's an Alberstons, a Unocal, a drive through for US Bank, a place called "Zack's Mechanical," and the Truck Stop Café. Mathew pulls into the café parking lot, turns off the ignition, and sits there looking at the yellow building with the steep green metal roof. At 11:30 in the morning the lot's plenty full. That means the café must be crowded. Where'd all these people come from? Mathew remembers the housing project he noticed a few miles back. From where he's sitting he can see two couples with silver hair in one of the booths near the window. His heart begins to race. Maybe this wasn't such a good idea after all. What if he can't find anyone who knows Allie Thompson. No, that's stupid. She worked at this café. But what if they think it's odd that he brought all this trash to show them. What if they're offended? What if they don't want it?

What if they think he's some kind of nut?

Sweat moistens his armpits. He looks in the rearview mirror and runs his fingers through his sandy gray hair, scowls at his shaggy eyebrows. He sits back and stares at the restaurant. A group of five are trouping inside. So, if he does go in, what is he going to do? He'll have to ask if anyone knows Allie Thompson. Who should he talk to? Who's going to be the most apt to treat this like business and not get all talky and familiar?

He fumbles with the keys, puts them back in the ignition, takes them out again. *Forget it. I'll look like a fool.*

As the engine rumbles to a start, visions of that night return—three faces looking up at him, pale in the starlight. He should have made them stay. He *was* a fool. With a jerk of his wrist he turns off the ignition, yanks out the keys, and throws them at the dashboard. He sits for a minute taking deep breaths. *Enough.* He gets out, goes around to the passenger side, and removes the trash sack. Holding it down at his side, he strides across the parking lot toward the entrance of the café. He stops. Now that he's closer he can see how crowded it is inside. A group standing near the door look like they're waiting for a table.

He's just about to turn around when he notices the sign in the window. "In loving memory of Allie, Sharon, and Joey Thompson…"

His hand is trembling and slick with sweat on the handle of the door. With what feels like the force of a thousand pound truck, he gives it a push and goes inside.

A Note From The Author

On August 3rd, 2011, while vacationing near Cameron Montana, my husband and I happened upon what was left of a tragic car accident that had occurred on the highway just up the hill from where we were staying. Swept into a pile by the side of the road were the remains of three lives. The sight has haunted me ever since. This story is dedicated to the memory of those who died: Gerri Kristine Anderson and her two children, Shelby Benito Anderson and Jacob William Anderson.

www.ingramcontent.com/pod-product-compliance
Lightning Source LLC
Chambersburg PA
CBHW021925170626
46807CB00007B/2983